What He Never Said

MARK FINDLAY SMITH

First published by Sharpe Books in 2021.

CONTENTS

Chapters 1 – 29
Author's Note

What's at the top of the stairs, lad?
What's at the top of the stairs?
Tell me what you see, lad,
Tell me what you see.
I see the man I fear sir,
I see the man I fear.
It is the man without a face sir,
The man without a face.

Traditional nursery rhyme

I suppose it was always going to be me who told the story of what happened to Sarah Brindle. JP certainly isn't going to do it, even though I've asked him to many times, and the other witnesses have either been killed or are in prison, so who else is there to trust? I also feel a certain responsibility, after everything that's happened, to make sure that all the facts are made public. And I hope, too, that I can change people's opinions about the case. You may believe you know men like me. You may even think we should be punished. But I am not ashamed. JP and I did what we did for the right reasons. We did what we thought was right.

Of course, there's a chance you may know the name Sarah Brindle already. It was a famous name once and I'm sure it will be again. The young actress murdered in the theatre. The killer who escaped into the streets. Gray's screams: *they're stabbing Sarah*. For days on end, the papers were filled with the lurid stories, about Sarah, her life, her friends, and the redoubtable Mrs R. But everything was changing then. Sarah was killed in the summer of 1914, in those first few weeks of the war when men – and boys who were desperate to be men – were heading in happy groups to the recruiting stations. Within weeks, the regretful letters … *we regret to inform you* … were arriving in their thousands, then their hundreds of thousands, and people forgot about the death of an actress back in 1914. I don't blame them really, when death became so commonplace.

As for JP, I'm not sure, even now, exactly what he went through in the war and what he saw and experienced at the Western Front, although I suspected from the moment we met that he'd been damaged in some way by it. I noticed the physical signs first. The scar that ran along his jawline. The way his hand sometimes trembled when he held a pen or lit a cigarette. And his eyes of course: the eyes that stared at something that wasn't there. Later, I learned about the scars I couldn't see, the scars beneath, which help explain our strange and memorable first meeting and much of what happened later. I wish I'd known then what I know now. Perhaps I could have done more to help my friend. If that's the right word. *Friend.*

Our first meeting was sometime late in 1918, not long after JP had been released from hospital. I discovered later that the doctors had again been trying everything they could to cure him. Sometimes, they would shine a bright light into his mouth and stare at the back of his throat in the search for a cause. Other times they would put him into solitary confinement. One doctor even told him there was no cure for a patient like him, a man who was a disgrace to the British army. No wonder JP was so withdrawn when we met. I can see him now: sitting low in his seat, hands thrust into the pockets of his coat. Pale. Thin. Silent.

Like me, JP's only ambition at the time was to resume his undergraduate studies and I don't remember him standing out particularly in the first few days. I think at some point I must have said hello to him and he didn't reply, but I didn't think much of it really. Then, about two weeks later, I was heading along the corridor towards the library when I saw him up ahead. He was standing against the wall. His head was turned down, and there was something about the angle of his body that was peculiar. The way his shoulders were stooped and turned in. I stopped and asked if he was ok. He didn't look up. I noticed his hands. The right one was holding tightly to the left which I could see was trembling. I asked if I could help, if there was anything I could do. He said nothing.

The fingers of his right hand were white with the pressure of trying to stop the left one shaking. I asked if I should fetch a doctor. I offered him a cigarette. He shook his head. It was the only acknowledgement he gave that I was there. I waited, but he did nothing. I think I must have spluttered "I'm Baker by the way, Harry Baker", but, after a few awkward minutes, I said I hoped he was OK and carried on up the corridor. What else could I do?

The following day, I happened to see him again in the morning, on the street outside the lecture halls, and, quite by instinct, asked him if he was feeling better. But again, he said nothing. Indeed, he seemed eager to avoid me and walked straight past without acknowledging I was there. It was extraordinary behaviour really, but I must admit it occurred to me that perhaps he knew who I was or had discovered the truth about me. But then I noticed that he was the same with everyone else too. He never spoke in lectures or, as far as I could tell, to any of the other students. He appeared to live a life, cut-off, in his own silent world.

I suppose I could have left it at that. I could have left JP in his wordless existence and thought no more about it. But the silence – and that trembling hand and his hopeless attempts to stop it – made me want to get through to him in some way, to help him if I could. Of course, we all talked about him at some point – in fact, he became a bit of a curiosity around the campus: the chap who never speaks. At one point, I asked one of my tutors, Professor Morrison, whether he knew JP, but when I raised the subject, the professor looked at me over his glasses, discomfited. 'Mr Allgood is a special case,' he said, 'and we are all to show as much consideration and … sympathy towards him as possible.' He looked down at his desk, a little awkwardly, like he knew more than he was saying.

As for the other students, they pretty much avoided JP – he was among us but not one of us. People either seemed to be disconcerted by his silence or couldn't be bothered making an effort. But there was something in me that thought: *keep trying.*

Exactly when the communication between the two of us moved on to the next stage I can't remember, but it was probably about two months into the term. We were sitting in class and JP had a novel with him, The Food of the Gods by HG Wells. Before I could change my mind, I scribbled a note about how much I liked the book and passed it to him. I watched him read the note and glance back at me. He picked up his pen. The hand. Just there. A tremble. He wrote something on the other side of the piece of paper and passed it back. *Excellent book*, it said, but it was signed as well. At the bottom of the page was his name in the handwriting I would come to know so well: *JP*. It felt like a step forward.

In the weeks after that, slowly at first, we kept the note-writing up. Obviously, I wanted to ask him why he never talked to anybody, and why he hadn't talked to me. But I kept to safe subjects – the lectures, books – and it became the way we communicated: the odd little note here and there. And in some ways, it felt *more* intimate than talking. After all, talking is what everyone does. JP and I had something different.

My fellow student Corie couldn't understand what I was doing. One day we were sitting in our favourite little tearoom after a lecture and when I raised the subject of JP, she cocked her head to one side and asked me why I was persisting in trying to be JP's friend when he didn't say anything. And I said 'I don't know, maybe he's lonely not talking to anyone, maybe he'd like a friend'. And Corie said he didn't look like he wanted a friend. But she hadn't seen him that day in the corridor, leaning against the wall, his head turned in, one hand holding tightly to another, skin turned white with the pressure.

It was the next day – the day after my chat with Corie – that JP sent me the note, the one that led to everything that happened next. I still have it in a drawer at home and I keep it because, really, the words changed the course of my life. There had been times in the early days of our acquaintance when I thought JP wanted to say something. A look would come over his face, strained, anxious, but it would pass. Other times, I'd glance up from my papers in a lecture and he'd be looking at me and it wasn't in a friendly way exactly. It was more calculating than that. But he would look away and the moment would pass. I know now that he was working out if I could be trusted. And that was when he passed me the note.

I can't say I noticed anything unusual about the day it happened. I was in the front row of the lecture hall and JP was sitting just along from me. When the lecture was over, everyone started to put their notes away, and I suppose I must have had my back turned at some point and that must have been when JP slipped the note into my papers. By the time I'd sorted through my things and put them away, JP had gone. I didn't think much of it and headed back to my rooms. I'd arranged to meet Corie in the evening, so when I got home, I put my bag on the chair by the door, changed, and headed out. JP's note – the 13 little words that would change my life – was still in my bag.

I recall what happened next very clearly. Corie and I went to the theatre and then a local dance hall and it was a pleasant evening. You could sense the mood in the streets in those days. The war was over and, although people had no money, and there were soldiers begging in the streets, and there were still men out in France waiting to come home, you could feel a kind of determination, a desperation, to get back to normal. We ended up in a little bar down the road from my rooms and Corie chatted away in that delightful way she has and as she did, I had a stab of conscience and guilt – *what kind of relationship does she really think we have?* But we sat in the booth at the back and lingered over a few cocktails and, as usual with Corie, I noticed that I felt less tense than I had before.

The following day, I was nursing a bit of a hangover and stayed in my rooms, looking at the newspaper and reading a book. I then did a bit of tidying up which is when I took my papers from my bag and put them on the desk. I noticed the piece of paper JP had passed to me, in the lecture hall. It was folded over, with no clue to its contents.

I can tell you now what the note said word for word. And what it looked like. And what I felt when I read it, the shock and confusion. Even now, even after all this time, even after the court case, and the newspaper stories, and the witnesses we talked to, and even after everything I know about the story of Sarah Brindle. And JP, standing in the corridor, watching it happen, watching her die.

JP's note read: *I don't know who else to tell. Someone is trying to kill me.*

2

Did I think JP was serious? Did I really think, when I read that extraordinary message that he believed someone was trying to kill him? It crossed my mind, obviously, that he was suffering terrors from the war – always in my mind was the sight of his white, trembling hand – but I wasn't sure. We had an eccentric relationship at that point, JP and I. We still do. We'd never actually spoken and yet now he was telling me someone was trying to kill him. I remember standing there for a few minutes, alone in my room, the note in my hand, uncertain what to make of it.

I sat on the bed and thought it through. Maybe it was some sort of joke. I looked at the words again: *someone is trying to kill me.* Who writes that sort of thing? Did he … did he mean it? I walked round the room, turning the paper over in my hand, and reading it and re-reading it. I realised I would have to seek JP out the next day and ask him what on earth he meant. Perhaps then he would tell me he'd been pulling my leg. Then I noticed how I was feeling: unsettled, like something had *shifted.*

The problem was: the next day JP wasn't there. The spot where he usually sat, near the front of the lecture hall, was empty, and it was empty again in the afternoon. It crossed my mind that I should speak to my tutors. The indecision nagged at me. *Someone is trying to kill me.*

I asked Corie about it over lunch at the tearoom.

'What do you make of this?' I said, passing the paper to her. She read it, slowly, while chewing.

'JP gave you this?' she said. 'How strange.' She passed it back to me. 'We thought he was *odd* and now we know for certain.'

'Yes, but do you think it's genuine?'

'Seems unlikely.'

'I'm not sure,' I said. 'I don't think he seems that sort. He's sensible.'

'You don't *know* him. You've never even spoken to him.'

'True, but we've got to know each other *a bit*.' I looked at the paper again. 'Maybe I should tell someone about it?'

'You could.' She sipped her tea. 'But have you tried *asking* him about it?' She raised her eyebrows. 'And has it crossed your mind that it could be a way of …' she paused and looked at me significantly from below her fringe '…attracting attention? From *you*?'

I shook my head. 'No,' I said. 'No one writes something like this unless they're serious. Do they? *Look at it.* I can't ignore it.' I put the note back in my pocket. 'I shall have to speak to him.'

Corie looked dubious. 'Good luck,' she said. She put a cigarette in her mouth and leaned across for me to light it.

The next day, JP was back in his usual place, sitting at the front of the room, as if everything was normal. He didn't look round when I came in. I sat down in the second row, leaned over and spoke to him quietly. I was aware some of the other students might hear. 'Can I talk to you about your message?' I said.

He glanced to his side and nodded. I told him I would meet him in the tearoom after the lecture.

When I got there, he was already sitting by the window. I ordered a cup of tea and sat down. JP barely looked at me. I added milk to my tea and watched it swirl and spread. How do you have tea with someone who doesn't talk? A couple of times I started to say something but faltered. JP took out a notebook, wrote a few words, and passed it to me. *I'm sorry I sent you the note. I couldn't think of anyone else.*

I read the words and looked at him. 'You do mean it then?' I said.

He nodded. We sat for a few more seconds, quiet. The steam rose from my tea. *Silence.*

I glanced round the tearoom, then leaned in closer. 'Someone is trying to kill you?' I said.

He nodded again.

I played with the teacup, turning it round in the saucer. I was aware of a young couple at a table nearby. He was leaning into her and trying to amuse her. She didn't look amused. I turned back to JP. 'Why would you think someone is trying to kill you?'

JP reached for his notebook but pulled back when one of the waitresses came to clear the table next to us. He then wrote carefully and slowly. *Someone tried to push me in front of a car.*

I looked at the words. 'Good God,' I said. 'Could it have been an accident?'

JP shook his head.

'What happened?' I asked. 'Were you hurt?'

JP shook his head again and wrote. *The car braked in time.*

'And you didn't see who it was? The man who pushed you?'

Again, a shake of the head.

'Have you told anyone about this?' I asked him. 'Have you reported it?'

JP looked hesitant, unsure of himself, then wrote a few words. *There is no one who can help.*

'I think we should go to the police,' I said. 'That's the obvious thing to do.'

JP took a sip of his tea. He peered at me over the cup. It felt like it was the first time he'd properly looked at me.

He put the cup down and for a second or two, his features seemed to tighten, as if he was trying to say something, to *will* the words out. Then the moment passed and he wrote another note. *I'm digging something up, otherwise they wouldn't have tried to kill me*

'They?' I said.

JP did not react. Behind us, the coffee machine spluttered. Plates clattered. Coins landed loudly in the cash register. The woman at the other table laughed. Perhaps her suitor was making process. Look at them, I thought, *talking*, like normal.

I straightened up and put my hands flat on the table. 'Look JP. I … want to help you, but how am I expected to if …' I fell silent. It was awkward. At the other table: laughter.

JP wrote a note. *I haven't been able to talk for a long time.*

I asked him if it was an injury, perhaps his throat was damaged when he was out at the Front, but he shook his head. It wasn't an injury. I asked him if he'd seen doctors, specialists, and he nodded. Had they been any help? A shake of his head again. At one point, I noticed, his hand went up to his throat and I thought: how fragile he is.

He wrote a note. *The doctors cannot work out what is wrong with me. Neither can I. I keep hearing and seeing things.*

'What kind of things?' I asked.

He flicked through his notebook and showed me the first page. On it, he'd written out the lines of a rhyme.

What's at the top of the stairs, lad?
What's at the top of the stairs?
Tell me what you see, lad,
Tell me what you see.

I see the man I fear sir,
I see the man I fear.
It is the man without a face sir,
The man without a face.

I recognised it, of course. It was the old nursery rhyme. I'd heard it sung a hundred times in the playground. It was in the book of rhymes I had as a child, although it was never one of my favourites. Rather macabre, I thought. My brother used to sing it to me to frighten me, but I never knew what it *meant*. Or why JP was showing it to me

'It's the old nursery rhyme,' I said to him. 'Weird little thing, isn't it? Why are so many nursery rhymes so peculiar?'

JP took the notebook back, turned to a fresh page, and wrote: *I keep hearing it in my head, and it's got something to do with what's happening to me.*

I asked him how and he shrugged. I sat back in the chair. I was trying to remember the tune. The tune to the rhyme. That's it. I started to hum. Cheerful little ditty really for something so dark. *What's at the top of the stairs, lad? What's at the top of the stairs?* I glanced at JP. I was still humming and I could see that it seemed to be having an effect on him. His face had gone white, ashen. His eyes had widened a little. He pushed back from the table, as if he was about to get up. The legs of his chair scraped on the floor, loudly, and the sound made the couple at the other table turn and look. I asked him if he was all right and he leaned forward and gripped the edge of the table. What an extraordinary person JP was. Was he normal, sane, had the war *driven him mad*?

I told him to have some more tea and he did. The man at the other table had gone back to his semi-effective wooing of the young lady. The coffee machine behind us hissed. It was all so normal, the sounds of a tearoom. And there was JP in the middle of it, silent.

I pulled the notebook towards me and started writing. 'Look,' I said, 'here's my address and telephone number. Write to me whenever you want … if you want to … if you find it … easier.' I pushed the notebook across the table. And as I did, something tapped at the back of my brain: *would JP want to write to you, or be your friend, if he knew who you really were?*

JP wrote his own address down, tore the page out, and passed it over to me. I looked at my watch and realised the time. We needed to be at the next lecture. JP put on his coat, straightened his tie, and smoothed down his hair. Neat, I thought. Ordered. Restrained. *Trapped*. He picked up the notebook and I thought of all the words in there, scribbled, and scrawled, and silent. We left. In the corner, the couple moved in closer to each other, and whispered.

3

I wasn't sure what to do next except wait for JP to make the next move. If I'm honest, there was part of me still that thought Corie might be right and JP was someone who made things up. There was every chance that, in the real world, no one had tried to push him under a car and that, when he went home every night, he sat and read his newspaper and led the same kind of dull life the rest of us did. But another part of me was curious and concerned. And perhaps I was also drawn to JP for another reason: I'm not normal either. Sometimes, I would sit in my rooms and I'd remember the shape of my old cell, the bed on one side, the small, high-up window, the chair, and I'd wonder what JP would do if he knew my story.

JP eventually made his next move three or four days after our meeting at the tearoom. I was coming out of the lecture hall and could see him just up ahead, waiting. He always stood out among other people because he looked so severe; so tall and shrouded in his great coat. He was standing about half-way down the corridor and when I reached him, he pushed a piece of paper into my hand and before I could say anything, he turned and walked away. I almost shouted after him, in frustration. I often felt like that in the early days, that I wouldn't be able to help him if he was so strange, so silent, so far away.

I looked at the note. *Please don't tell anyone about the contents of this message. You asked why someone would want to kill me. It's because of what I saw. What my friend Gray and I saw. At the theatre. We saw Sarah Brindle stabbed to death. It happened in front of us. Then Gray died, under the wheels of a tram. I wonder if he was pushed. And I wonder if the person who pushed him tried to do the same to me. I must find out what happened. But I need your help. I meant what I said: someone is trying to kill me. JP.*

I read and re-read the words a few times, the other students filing past me. I went to the tearoom and read it again (the courting couple were back at the other table, I noticed). Then I went back to my rooms and lay on my bed and read the message for the 20th, 30th, 100th time. The question was: what should I *do*? I went to my desk and wrote a reply to JP, asking him to come and see me. I would send it the next day and perhaps JP and I could come to a resolution about the action we should take. I was still feeling a mixture of interest and anxiety. I paced round my room for a bit, looked out of the window for signs of life, opened a book, closed it, then pulled the suitcase out from under the bed and sought comfort from the things I hid there.

JP came to my rooms about three days later and it was awkward at first. He sat in the chair by the window and I made him some tea and sat on the bed across from him. Have you ever sat down with someone who says nothing at all? You suddenly realise that one way we get through our days is by filling them with words – *words, words, words* – but when someone doesn't play the game, like JP, it strikes you how shallow so much of it is. At first, as I moved around the room and made the tea, I made light-hearted remarks about my rooms, or my landlady, or our lectures, and JP would try to raise the beginnings of a smile. But I always noticed the same thing: it was never enough to banish the melancholy.

Eventually, after we'd drunk our tea, I put my cup down, and clasped my hands together. 'You need to tell me how I can help,' I said.

He reached into one of the deep pockets of his coat and took out his black notebook. He opened it and started writing. He took his time. He didn't seem particularly self-conscious about the act of writing and the silence that went with it. He leaned over and showed me what he'd written. *It will probably be DANGEROUS.* He'd written the last word in capital letters. I noticed his dark eyes again, unmoving in the pale, thin face. *DANGEROUS.*

I sat back in my chair. I noticed the sounds of the street outside. A car going past. A door closing. Two women talking, their voices getting louder then quieter again as they passed by. JP had started writing again and, in short, sharp, notes, explained what he wanted to do. He wanted to find out the truth about Sarah Brindle. He wanted to speak to the people who knew her. Her friends. His friends. I asked why he was coming to me for help rather than one of his friends and he wrote six sharp words on the paper: *because I do not trust them.* After a couple of minutes, he dug around in his pockets again until he found what he was looking for and placed it on the bed next to me. A photograph. A group of children. Gathered at the front of a classroom. They were all about 15 or 16 years old. Their names were written along the bottom of the picture, along with the date: 1909. JP pointed to a girl in the middle of the photograph, and I knew at once who it must be. *Sarah Brindle.*

I looked at her more closely. She looked confident. Black hair cut into a bob, head thrust forward; she was smiling. She was arm in arm with a girl to her right. The girl's name was written underneath. *Elizabeth Mackie.*

'And there's you,' I said, pointing to a thin boy at the back of the picture. Standing next to him was a shorter boy with blond hair. *Gray Ritchie.* The boy who'd witnessed the murder with JP. To their left were two girls. *Barbara.*

Rachel. Barbara dark with a lively face; Rachel more withdrawn. They were looking at each other earnestly. Behind them was a thin, slightly frowning boy. *Daniel*. It was a picture of seven rather ordinary-looking children. But two of them had died. *Sarah*. And then another. *Gray*.

JP took the picture back and looked at it for a few seconds. He was holding the photograph in front of him and as he leaned slightly into the light from the window, I noticed his hand was trembling again. What had he seen in France? What had it done to his body? *And his mind?*

This might have been the moment when any right-thinking person would have realised it was all too much. JP was not a well man, and he appeared to have obsessions which might or might not be fantasies. A reasonable person might have told JP they couldn't get involved and he should go to the police, or a doctor. And they might also think: who is this man? The man is afraid of his friends. He is obsessed with a curious old rhyme. He thinks someone is trying to kill him. He never speaks. But in that moment in front of the window, in my modest rooms, with JP sitting there, looking at the picture, his hand trembling and hinting at what might have happened, I only felt great compassion for him. I wanted to help. I picked up his notebook, which he'd placed on the little table, and I wonder, when I think back, why I chose to do what I did. I didn't speak to him in that moment and I think it was my way of trying to get closer to my new friend, of showing him I wanted to understand what he was going through. I straightened the notebook in front of me, wrote a message on the clean, white paper, and showed it to JP. *Tell me what you'd like me to do.*

4

I spent quite a few days worrying about what would happen next. In those early weeks, I was already taking on some of the fear and anxiety of the situation. It also didn't help that I had other concerns. Perhaps someone would discover the pictures and letters that were hidden under my bed. Perhaps someone would see where I go at night. And maybe someone from my past would see me in the street, or at university, and point a finger and say: *I know who you are.* I had a feeling that JP might be able to help me, just as I might be able to help him, but, for now, I didn't know how.

While I was waiting for JP to get in touch again, Corie and I went out for tea and drinks a couple of times. But there was something that held me back from confiding in her fully. Perhaps it was my knowledge that I wasn't the kind of person she thought I was. I think I was afraid, as I always was, that she would stop talking to me if I was truthful; I was also worried that she might come across an old newspaper with my name in it, or simply hear a piece of gossip whispered in her ear about the man she thought was her friend.

And when I wasn't with anyone, when I was in my room, lying on the bed, smoking a cigarette, or pretending to read one of my textbooks, little snippets and phrases from the past few days would come back to me and the extraordinary thing was: it wasn't like normal memories: I didn't hear the words in my head, I saw them written down on bits of paper. *Someone is trying to kill me. What's at the top of the stairs, lad? It's the man without a face.* Then I would remember people at school singing that strange song. Sometimes, I'd hum it to myself. Then I'd stop because I realised it was making me feel like it used to make me feel as a child: unpleasant, a little uncertain, fearful.

The next time I saw JP was at a lecture a few days after he'd visited my rooms. He looked even more intense than ever, sitting in the front row, back upright, his dark eyes forward and unmoving. He kept going into the pockets of his big black coat, taking pens out, then putting them back in again. Fussing. Once or twice, he glanced across at me. But just a glance.

I caught up with him as we were leaving. He took a piece of paper from his pocket. He'd written something on it. He stood in front of me while I read it. *I'm going back to the theatre. Will you come?*

I didn't quite understand what he meant.

'The theatre?' I said.

JP nodded. He moved aside to let some other students get past.

Then I realised. *The theatre.* Where it happened. Where Sarah Brindle was killed. 'Should we do that?' I said.

JP didn't nod or shake his head. He just looked at me. I would get used to the expression, that look on his face. He had the most extraordinary eyes: dark in a pale frame; intense, powerful, and *convincing*. So, even though I still hadn't worked out what I thought about the whole affair, I said yes, I would go to the theatre with him. Perhaps this was the moment when I was really pulled in. I now know where my decision to help JP led: the exposed secrets, including my own, the violence, the blood. But I do not regret it. I *mustn't* regret it. I said yes I would meet him at the theatre. JP wrote down a time. *8pm.*

When I got there later that night, JP was standing by the front entrance. What I wasn't expecting was the fact he had a dog with him. A pretty little thing. Collie, a little bit of spaniel. Brown with specks of white. As I approached, the dog strained forward, tail wagging and sniffed at my hand, her eyes turned up to me. Why was I surprised that JP had a dog? When I thought about it afterwards, I realised I shouldn't be surprised at all: he was more relaxed around her and, of course, there was another reason when I thought about it: you don't have to *talk* to dogs to be able to communicate with them. I discovered later her name was Moll.

With Moll pulling ahead, JP led the way round the back of the building to the stage door. It was open. Inside, there was a man, chubby and grey, sitting in the reception area, smoking a cigarette and reading a newspaper through the cloud of smoke. He glanced up and spotted JP and didn't seem surprised to see him. He gave a little nod, then looked back down at the paper. Did JP know him? I followed JP inside and we went up the stairs that led into the building.

A thought occurred to me, a thought I was little ashamed of: *was I safe?* Would JP take me into this theatre and suddenly turn on me? I had to push the thought down and tell myself to be reasonable. The building, the lack of light, the smell of dust and paint, weren't helping. And as we went deeper into the building, I knew why: the windowless walls, the bricks, they reminded me of my recent past: the island, the cold, *prison.*

The stairs from the stage door led to a long corridor. On one side, there were some dressing rooms; on the other, rooms for storage. One of the doors was open, and I could see a cluster of props and structures; the remnants of old plays and shows. At the end of the corridor was another flight of stairs. JP took them two at a time. I wondered if it was just me who could suddenly hear the old rhyme in my head again. *What's at the top of the stairs, lad?* Was JP feeling it? I followed him to the top. *Tell me what you see, lad. Tell me what you see.*

'This is it?' I asked when we'd reached the top. There was another corridor in front of us, about 30 or 40ft long.

JP showed no sign of moving. It was dusty and messy up here – it was obvious the theatre folk didn't use the place much. I could hear the roof rattling; it was getting windy outside. Maybe it was my imagination but I thought I was starting to hear things more intensely when I was with JP, as if I was finely tuned to the moments that broke the silence. At the end of the corridor was the door to a room. I looked at JP.

'Are you okay?' I asked. I didn't feel quite myself. I didn't feel *right*.

JP nodded, barely, then headed down the corridor. The door to the room was open. He stepped inside. I followed him. Moll sniffed in the corners. This was the place where Sarah Brindle was killed. It looked fairly ordinary. A smallish room. About 20ft by 20ft. There was one window in the far wall and boxes and packing cases along the other walls. I could see that it was used for storage. In the box nearest to us, there were flashes of colour spilling out. Costumes? On the shelves above were props and curious bits of bric-a-brac that had once been used in plays perhaps. A lamp. Vases. Masks. JP stepped further into the room and put his hand on the wall. He turned and looked round at the floor, taking it in.

I didn't know what to say. JP took another couple of steps forward, then turned to me. I wasn't sure what he wanted me to do, but it seemed he wanted me to come further in. That thought again: *was I safe?* Once I was closer in, he raised his hand and indicated that he wanted me to stay where I was. Then he put his hands on my arm again and moved me slightly to the left. I was facing into the room, with my back to the door. JP stood looking at me intently for a few seconds, then seemed happy with what he saw.

'Is there something wrong?' I asked. JP shook his head. 'You want me to stay here?' I said. He walked past me and left the room and I could hear him, but not see him, walking down the corridor. I stayed where I was. I could hear JP moving around, his feet scuffing on the floor. I could hear the dog sniffing the ground, her claws on the stone. I did not move. After a couple of minutes or so, JP came back down the corridor, and put his hand on my arm as a sign that it was okay for me to move. I'd only been standing there for a minute or two, but it felt like longer.

I turned to JP. He was standing by the door, facing in. The light from the window had fallen across his eyes. I thought: he's not really here, is he? He's back there, years ago, in the room when it happened. He started rummaging in his pockets and took out his notebook. He wrote in it. *Something isn't the same as before.*

I looked around. 'You mean something has changed about the room?' I asked.

JP headed up the corridor again, Moll trotting next to him. He stopped near the top of the stairs. I walked towards him. 'Has being here helped?' I asked.

He looked back down at the room. His eyes narrowed. Was he playing the scene in his head again? What happened here? After a couple of minutes, he closed his eyes and rubbed at them with his fingers.

I'm not sure how long we stayed there, up in the theatre. It can't have been more than about 10 minutes. It's fanciful really, but I wondered if the fact that JP didn't speak might have enhanced his other abilities. I watched him standing there, narrowing his eyes and turning his pen over and over in his hand. Could he see what he saw that day? Could he feel it? I didn't say anything. We were both silent. For a few minutes we were both mute witnesses. Then JP seemed to snap out of his reverie and, without looking at me, he turned and made his way back down the stairs.

5

There was something about our visit to the theatre that helped me make my mind up about JP and what he had asked me to do. JP was the most extraordinary – and disturbing – person I'd ever met and I still had no idea what the real reasons for his silence were. But the fact that he'd asked me to come with him to the theatre that night demonstrated a trust in me. I was beginning to realise he had very few people to turn to. I had to help him, even if I didn't completely understand why.

It was just as I was making this resolution that JP took me to one side after one of our lectures. Our visit to the theatre had been playing in my mind for some days, but, as usual, my instincts told me to wait for JP to make a move rather than push him to reveal more than he was ready to. Just as we were leaving the lecture, he put his hand on my shoulder as a signal to wait and handed me an envelope. He then put his hand over mine and squeezed it and I understood. Whatever he'd given me was important. He fixed me with a firm look, then turned and left.

It was only when everyone had left the lecture hall and I was alone that I opened the envelope and looked at its contents. Inside were newspaper cuttings. I took a couple of them out and looked at them. GIRL STABBED TO DEATH IN THEATRE. HUNT GOES ON FOR KILLER. And other lurid headlines. One of the cuttings in particular caught my eye. There was a picture of a young woman. The caption read: *Miss Sarah Brindle, actress.* It was the first time I'd seen a picture of Miss Brindle as a grown woman. It appeared to have been taken in a photographic studio. She had a hand up to her chin and her face was pressed forward, her eyes up to the camera. It wasn't exactly a smile on her face, more the beginnings of one. I felt a pang of melancholy. She was so young, and rather beautiful, and she could have had a future.

Above the picture was a headline in ink-black capitals. THEATRE MURDER: WITNESSES' ORDEAL and the story read as follows:

'Further to the terrible murder of the actress Miss Sarah Brindle this week, The Daily Herald can reveal the dramatic ordeal of the witnesses to the crime.

Mr JP Allgood and Mr Gray Ritchie were visiting their friend at His Majesty's Theatre when the tragedy occurred. Miss Brindle, who is a member of the repertory company at His Majesty's, was preparing for a play to be performed the following evening.

Mr Gray Ritchie told the Daily Herald that he and Mr Allgood had arrived at the theatre and were searching for Miss Brindle. It was at that moment they heard screams.

According to Mr Allgood, the two men ran upstairs and witnessed the murder taking place. They saw, through an open door at the end of a corridor, a man standing over Miss Brindle and stabbing her. The man was wearing a gown and a mask.

'We ran forward at once, but the murderer stood up, slammed the door and locked it before we could do anything,' said Mr Ritchie. 'We attempted to break the door down with no success.'

Mr Allgood then ran down the stairs to fetch help and it was his good fortune to see two police constables further along the street. Within a few minutes, Mr Allgood and the constables had reached the top of the theatre again and, between them, the four men managed to break the door down. They found the unfortunate Miss Brindle, dead or dying, on the other side of the door.

The police officer in charge of the case, Chief Inspector Downs, said his investigations were continuing and that the testimony of Mr Allgood and Mr Ritchie had been valuable. 'These two gentlemen had the misfortune to witness a murder happen in front of their eyes,' said Chief Inspector Downs, 'but it is greatly to be hoped that their accounts will be most helpful in tracking down the culprit.'

I read through the other cuttings and, collectively, they gave me a good impression of what happened. Gray and JP told one of the newspapers that the man who killed Sarah had been wearing a long purple gown that came down to the floor and covered his whole body. Gray described it as resembling a priest's garment. JP thought it might have been a costume. It was later discovered stuffed into one of the boxes in the room and was identified by the theatre staff as a costume they had previously used in a play.

The newspapers also said it was discovered later how the murderer had escaped. The mask he had been wearing was found on the ground in the street behind the theatre and Chief Inspector Downs speculated that the murderer had left by the window, climbed down over the roofs and into the street and discarded his mask on the way. One of the newspapers published a picture of the mask and it was a rather grisly thing. It was completely black with two holes for the eyes. I was rather disturbed by the eyes, staring blankly from the page.

I sat and read and re-read the cuttings for some time. No wonder JP was so affected, and upset, by our visit to the theatre. What a terrible experience he had been through, and his friend Gray. I thought back to the corridor and the room beyond. I am a religious man, a man of God, and I like to think that the good book has guided me for most of my life, but I am not a superstitious man. I do not believe in ghosts. But I was affected by the atmosphere in that place and now I could imagine the grisly details of what happened there. Gray and JP standing there and catching a glimpse, before the door was slammed in their faces, of someone killing their friend.

Some of the other cuttings were from the weeks and months following the murder. Chief Inspector Downs was recorded a couple of times saying the investigation was ongoing. Another story said there had been a witness who had found the mask in the street. And then, at the bottom of the pile, I came across a final cutting. Much smaller. Just a few paragraphs.

IDENTITY OF MAN KILLED IN TRAM ACCIDENT: A young man who died after being hit by a tram has been identified as Mr Gray Ritchie. Mr Ritchie was killed on the corner of Campbell Street on May 24th. The Transport Corporation said they deeply regretted the death of the young man and that an investigation was being conducted.

This was the second death JP had told me about. First, his friend Sarah is murdered. Then Gray is hit by a tram or … was pushed under the tram? That's what JP had told me, wasn't it? *I wonder if he was pushed. And I wonder if the person who pushed him tried to do the same to me.* I looked back through the cuttings, at the lurid headlines, and the pictures of Sarah Brindle, bright-eyed, happy. The stories described her as a popular woman and a promising actress. The manager of the theatre said she'd had a great future ahead of her. A future ended by a knife, I thought.

When I got home, I put the cuttings away in a drawer and

wrote to JP, telling him I'd read the newspaper stories and was ready to do whatever he wanted to do. A couple of days later, I got a reply. He told me he'd written some time ago to all the people he'd like to meet and would set up appointments. He thanked me again, in that spindly handwriting of his, but he ended the note with another warning: *do not talk to anyone about this.*

6

I think it was a week or so later that I received a short message from JP saying he had set up a visit to Miss Brindle's friend Elizabeth Mackie. I was nervous of course. First, I wasn't sure I had the *right* to ask questions of the friends of Sarah Brindle. Second, I was anxious about how the meeting would go. I had a horror that we might all sit there in complete silence. And third, I was worried about JP, and myself as well a little. I remembered the words JP had written in my rooms and the last word, in capitals: *DANGEROUS*.

The visit was set up for the following week and JP, with Moll the dog, and I met each other at the end of the road where Miss Mackie has a small flat. JP had told me one or two details about her in his note. She had trained as a nurse and during the war had served in one of the field hospitals in France and now she was back and working at the cottage hospital.

Miss Mackie's rooms were in a big, rather ugly building on the corner of the road near the entrance to a park. When we arrived, she fussed over Moll, scratching behind her ears, and made us tea in neat little teacups and sat on the edge of her settee.

'It's good to see you JP,' she said. She said that she was terribly sorry to hear that he had been in hospital after the war and that he'd been …. injured. She wasn't quite sure how to refer to the fact that JP was silent and so she talked a little instead about her experiences in France, her months in the hospital camp and it was always with the kind of calm detachment I'd noticed in other men and women who'd been out there.

Eventually, she stopped talking and looked at me expectantly, her eyes narrow under her straight-line fringe. A little awkwardly at first, I said that JP was unhappy that the murder of Sarah Brindle remained unsolved and he wanted to do what he could to find out what happened and I, Harry Baker, his friend, was going to help him. Was that OK? Miss Mackie put her hand out to her teacup, then withdrew it again. I could tell she was cautious. She'd never met me before and yet here I was in her rooms acting as some sort of spokesman for JP. She asked a few questions about who I was and I was aware of the familiar thought at the back of my brain: *don't ask me about the war.* JP wrote a few notes telling Miss Mackie that I was his friend and she could trust me and, in the end, she said she would do whatever she could. I loved Sarah, she said. That word: *loved.* I found out later she meant it. Not liked. *Loved.*

And so Elizabeth Mackie sat on the edge of the settee, serious, earnest, and told us about her experiences of the day Sarah died. She talked a little about what kind of woman Sarah was, and I thought back to that picture of her in the newspaper. She was so lively and bright, said Miss Mackie, and determined to become an actress despite the disapproval of her parents. That was the thing about Sarah, said Miss Mackie: she was strong-willed, but she was never arrogant. She made decisions and, when she thought they were right, she stuck to them.

Miss Mackie also told us that, on the day Miss Brindle died, she had seen her in the morning and the young actress was terribly excited about taking part in the play the following day. However, Miss Mackie also remembered that her friend had occasionally seemed distracted. There was always a bit of that when you are friends with one of the most popular girls in the school, she said, but it was never meant in a bad way. Sarah Brindle was a lovely person, a beautiful person.

I asked her how Miss Brindle's death had affected her. Badly, she said. She had remained in her rooms for some weeks, partly because she was frightened about her own safety – the murder had been grotesque and horrible and the culprit was not caught – but mostly because she couldn't believe that Sarah – bright, shining Sarah – was dead. I asked if she might have a theory about who might have committed the crime. Not at all, she said. It was probably a boy; there were a few on the go most of the time with Sarah and she'd been upset when Gray had ended their relationship. But Miss Mackie said she'd wished Sarah had realised that boys aren't everything.

We kept on talking, with JP a silent presence. Occasionally, he would pass a piece of paper to Miss Mackie with a question. It crossed my mind that JP's presence had a peculiar effect that I would notice more and more in the coming weeks: he did not speak and it seemed to encourage other people to speak *more,* at first to fill the silence, but then I wondered if it made it easier for them to just talk and *reveal*.

Miss Mackie put her tea on the table beside the settee. 'JP ... I ... I'm so sorry about what's happened.' She shifted in her seat and didn't say it, but we knew she meant the fact JP didn't speak. 'We've both been badly affected by this haven't we? But I have, *slowly*, been able to get back to an ordinary life. Do you think ...' her sentence drifted into silence and JP wasn't going to fill it.

I think I said something – I can't remember what – and Miss Mackie then talked a little more about her experiences in France. She had seen so many wounded men, she said, every day, and so many dead men, and treating people in the cottage hospital for broken legs and the Spanish Flu seemed normal in comparison. And as she talked, I felt a familiar agony about whether I'd done the right thing. I could feel the small metal label that I kept, always, secretly, in my pocket. A reminder. A number. 8161. And the question occurred to me again: what was I doing here, *really*?

We drifted into pleasantries before Miss Mackie told us she must report to the hospital so I thanked her and left. Back out in the street, JP raised his hand as if in thanks then walked away down the street, Moll beside him. I felt a flash of irritation: what the hell was going on here? I was now involved in the mystery of this man's life and he hadn't even said a word to me, *ever*. Maybe it was understandable that he wouldn't speak to anyone, but why wouldn't he speak to me? He turned a corner and was gone.

A couple of days later, to my surprise, I received a letter from Miss Mackie. She said she hoped I didn't mind, but could we meet up again? She'd like to talk to me without JP being there. And I thought: *what could this be?* I wrote back and said yes, and the next week, I went to her rooms and she suggested a walk in the park. She told me how uncomfortable she'd felt at first about the situation, about JP not speaking. And then she began to talk about Sarah.

'It's odd,' she said. 'I didn't really know why Sarah was my friend.'

'Why do you say that?' I asked.

'Because I was the odd child, the serious one. And I was never … fashionable, like Sarah. My mother cut my hair and bought clothes because they were cheap. What has JP told you about Sarah?'

'Not all that much.'

'He probably hasn't told you that her family had no money. None of us had money really, but I think it was a real struggle for Sarah sometimes. She tried to hide it, but it was.' Miss Mackie stopped by the duck pond and looked into the water. She told me more about Miss Brindle: how her father had died when she was a baby and how her mother had been diagnosed with a muscular disease when she was in her forties and then Miss Brindle was killed and within two years Miss Brindle's mother was dead too. And that's how it happens, and how quickly it happens: a family is there, and then it isn't. And the fighting, hundreds of miles away in France, had nothing to do with it, for a change.

'You and Sarah were good friends?' I said. 'That must've helped you both.'

Miss Mackie shrugged her shoulders. 'I'm not sure really but I sometimes wondered if she felt sorry for me, because there was a profoundly caring side to her; you could see that with her mother when she fell ill.' She looked into the pond again. 'That's why I didn't understand it when she died. I know I said all this to JP the other day, but my first thought was: it must be a special friend, a boyfriend. Whoever it was, he or she was wearing a mask, weren't they?'

We'd reached a park bench near the gate and Miss Mackie asked me if I wanted to sit for a bit. We did and there was quiet between us for a while. I was getting more and more used to silences.

'JP thinks someone is trying to kill him,' I said.

She looked at me sharply.

'He says someone tried to push him under a car.'

'Why? Why would they do that?' she said.

'He thinks it might be because he's been asking questions about the murder.' I felt a stab of guilt: should I be telling Miss Mackie this? I remembered JP's appeal: *do not talk to anyone about this.*

She was silent for a second or two. 'That's frightening. That really happened?' I told her what JP had told me and she shook her head as she listened.

'If someone's after JP, he should go to the police,' she said. 'They never caught whoever killed Sarah. He's still around, somewhere.'

'He won't go to the police,' I said.

'Then why are you getting involved?' She put a hand on my knee. 'If there's danger, you're putting yourself in the path of it.' She took her hand off my knee. 'All of us.'

'I suppose I am, but I couldn't say no. Even though JP doesn't talk, he's persuasive.'

Elizabeth smiled, although I could see she was still a little unsettled. 'Even though JP never said much at school, and was *serious*, there was always something attractive about him,' she said. 'The difference maybe. He didn't love sports or the traditional things other boys like. He liked books. And he was *intense*.' The sun had moved behind a cloud and changed the colour of the trees from green to black. A duck made its way across the pond. Elizabeth looked back at me. 'What has JP told you about himself?'

'Only that he was a witness. We went back to the theatre, where it happened.' She raised her eyebrows and I told her about our visit: in through the stage door, along the corridor, past the room with the rows of masks staring out at us, up the stairs – *what's at the top of the stairs, lad?* – then the corridor and through the door: the room where Sarah Brindle died.

Miss Mackie listened and asked the obvious question – was it wise to go back to the theatre? – then another thought occurred to her. 'I think there could be something more personal going on,' she said.

'What do you mean?' My body had tensed up.

'They were quite a tight-knit little group you know,' said Elizabeth. 'Gray and JP and Sarah and I didn't particularly like it, towards the end. It was intense, but it was as if they couldn't see it themselves.'

'In what way?'

'Well, Gray obviously liked Sarah and I always thought that maybe … JP was fond of Gray.' She looked at me seriously and kept her eyes on mine. 'Gray and JP had an odd relationship in a way,' she said. 'Unexpected I mean. I think he was rather scared by Gray at first, I think we all were. He wasn't a bad boy, just a bit of a bully, as some boys can be. He would play practical jokes, you know, and laugh at people, and throw his weight around with the boys who were weaker or different, like JP.'

She looked out across the duck pond. 'I remember one time, there was a fight in the playground. Between Gray and JP, I mean. We must have been nine or ten. Young. You know what kids are like, we all gathered round JP and Gray as they sort of grappled on the floor; it was nothing serious. But suddenly, JP started to get the better of Gray. Gray was a bit of a bully but JP was taller and bigger and it was if JP suddenly realised his own strength. After a minute or two, he had Gray pinned down and he said to him 'what are you going to do now eh?' And Gray laughed and they got up, and I think that was probably a turning point in their relationship. After that, they were firm friends.'

I looked at her. She was lost in the past. 'I can't imagine,' I said, 'what it could be like, for JP. He lost Miss Brindle and then Gray and then he went out to France and must have lost … so many friends.'

She turned and looked at me. 'Has he told you much?' she said.

I shook my head.

'No, they never do,' she said. 'JP signed up in the first wave in August and we wrote to each other a few times, particularly when I was out in France myself, in the hospitals. The thing is the letters are so *anodyne,* but one learns to read between the lines. And I saw the injuries myself. The men without limbs, without eyes, *without faces,* and JP was injured too but not in the same way. His injuries are hidden, under the flesh and the bone.'

She kept looking out over the pond. 'You know, I sometimes wonder if JP signed up because of Gray.'

I asked her what she meant. 'I'm not sure,' she said. 'It's just that Sarah was murdered, and then Gray got into trouble, and then he was hit by the tram and died, and when the war broke out, perhaps JP thought: what have I got to lose?' She turned to me. 'JP has seen *so much death* Mr Baker.'

'What do you mean by Gray getting into trouble,' I asked.

She sighed. 'Drugs,' she said. 'We all lost touch with him really, when it got very bad, but there is a thought that he was hit by the tram because he was … you know, in the thrall of drugs at the time.'

'I didn't realise that,' I said. 'Perhaps the murder of his friend…'

Miss Mackie nodded. 'I'm sure. There is never only one victim of a murder. There's the person who's killed, but then there's the people who saw it, or the family of the victim, their mother, their father, their friends, like JP. It would explain JP's determination to find out who did it, wouldn't it? JP does get obsessed about things and that's a good quality but it's a bad quality too. I became a bit wary of them, those three.'

'Do you think the killer might have been jealous of one of them … or something else?'

'Sarah had a few boyfriends. Like Dan. Have you met Dan?'

'I think we're going to at some point.'

'I was a friend of Sarah, but I was always slightly on the edge of it. Boys didn't like me. Not that I care now.' She looked at me intently again. I said nothing. 'Why are you getting involved in this, *really*?' she asked.

'JP asked me.'

'Yes, I know, but you barely know him.'

'He asked me for help, and I said yes.'

'The thing is, I don't think JP is always honest. That's what I wanted to tell you. He might not have told you everything.'

I asked her what she meant.

'You hear things,' she said, 'and I think there was another reason Gray and JP and Sarah formed that little group because all of them, in a way, had problems.'

'JP not talking you mean?'

'No, I mean long before that. He had an unusual family you know. He never invited us back to the house, but I met his mother and father a couple of times and I can see where he gets his intensity from. There was something about them that made me tense, awkward.'

I suddenly had a thought about what might be going on. 'Are you warning me against JP?'

'No ... It's just that I could see that you – I hope you don't mind me saying – are quite attached to JP already and JP is not ... conventional. *Normal*.' She put her hand up and brushed at her hair. It had turned a little cold, and a little dark. The birds had gone. She told me what JP had said in some of his letters from the front. How he missed the sounds of home – the trams, crowds of people, the newspaper boy at the corner calling out the headlines. But he'd said something else in his letters. He missed the silence too. And then he'd written from hospital, when he got back home – just one letter, before they stopped completely, and he told her how the doctors had given him tablets and made him run up and down in the grounds of the hospital and one of them had even shouted at him and told him he was a disgrace to the army and to his country, and, in his letter to Elizabeth, JP had said: *I don't need a doctor to tell me that.* And JP told her that none of the treatments were working and how he'd grown to like the quiet, the lack of words, and needed it. *I couldn't find the words to describe how I was feeling and then I couldn't find the words at all.*

Miss Mackie said it was starting to get dark and they should go. 'I hope you don't think I'm unsympathetic Mr Baker, but sometimes, don't you think, there's something else about the fact that JP doesn't speak. Something unpleasant, I mean. A kind of arrogance. Don't you think?' She got up and looked out over the pond again. 'I *would* like to help you know. I want to know who killed my friend.' She turned to me. 'But listen. I *am* thinking about going to the police about this.'

I told her I understood that.

'If you ask me,' she went on, 'you should have gone to the police already if people are getting pushed under cars. He was all right wasn't he? JP, I mean. He wasn't hurt?'

'The car braked in time, but he could've been killed.'

She shook her head again. 'What the *hell* is going on?'

I stood up and brushed down my trousers. 'Listen,' she said, 'I want you to get in touch whenever you want. With JP …' she looked at me significantly … 'or without.' She started walking towards the gate. It had gone very quiet. Apart from … what? The sound of our shoes on the ground. Something in the branches above us, moving the leaves. Some traffic, in the distance. And a tune in my head. That wretched tune. The notes tapped on the inside of my brain. Tap. Tap. An old tune. Tap. The old nursery rhyme. Tap. Tap. *Tell me what you see.* Tap.

7

I didn't tell JP about my meeting with Elizabeth Mackie for quite some time and I'm not sure why. Perhaps it was something to do with what Miss Mackie said about my new friend, that he might not be telling me everything he knew. But I also realised that, although I was willing to help JP, I had to be cautious and protect my own interests as well. A week or so after the meeting, JP wrote to me to tell me he'd set up another meeting, this time with Gray's mother. I thought back to the photograph JP had shown me of the tight little group of friends, with Gray in the middle, frowning slightly from under his mop of blonde hair. And I thought of what Miss Mackie had said, about what happened when the little boy grew up: the drugs, then the wheels of the tram.

Gray's mother – known to everyone as Mrs R – lived in a handsome red sandstone villa at the end of a long line of houses, not far from the theatre. I wondered what to expect. Would Mrs R welcome JP, and his friend, coming to her house and asking questions? As it happens, she couldn't have been more friendly or solicitous. Indeed, she seemed pleased to see JP and seemed to know already about his injuries and his condition. JP had also brought Moll the dog with him which provided a useful distraction; Mrs R fussed over the dog and gave her biscuits. She also filled the quiet left by JP with chitter-chatter, about the house, and the war, and what would happen next, and all those soldiers coming home and no work for them, and wasn't it a tragedy, and how had he been and other inconsequential bits and pieces, made all the more awkward by the fact JP never replied to any of it. And then, once she'd chatted and made us tea, and given Moll another biscuit or two, and arranged cake on a plate and pressed a few slices on us, she sat back in her chair and the air seemed to go out of her a bit, like she couldn't keep it up.

We sat for a few moments, saying nothing. Suddenly, Mrs R seemed a little bit lost in her voluminous dress. She was a thin woman; you could see the bones in her face and in her fingers. Black lace covered her neck and there was more of it in the hair that was pulled back from her long, thin face. Her fingers picked at the arm of the chair and I noticed little details of the room. A bowl of sweet peas and roses on the mantelpiece. A bible on the table by her chair. Pictures of Gray on the sideboard. The photographs showed him progressing from boy to young man. In the later ones, his face was drawn, the smile a little forced.

Mrs R seemed to notice me looking at the pictures and picked one up. Gray was a little older, 17 perhaps, maybe 18, and was wearing some sort of sporting uniform. He was holding up a trophy of some kind. Mrs R sat for a minute or two looking at it, then she smiled and looked up at us.

'I hope you don't mind me saying gentlemen, but these pictures are not a source of sadness to me. Not really. Because we know that my son is not dead.' She put the photograph back in its place and reached out to the bible on the table and rested a hand on it. 'I think of the words from Corinthians,' she said. '*The truth is that Christ has been raised from death, as the guarantee that those who sleep in death will also be raised.* Those words are a constant comfort to me.'

She turned to me. 'Have you ever been to a spiritualist church Mr Baker?'

I said that I hadn't. 'The spiritualist church is a great

comfort to me,' she said. She put a hand up to the lace at her neck. 'Mrs Ribble may be a source of scorn for some, or fear even, but she is one of the country's finest mediums, and I have come to rely on her, and her services, a great deal. My son did not die.'

I wasn't quite sure what to say so I asked about the pictures on the sideboard and Mrs R seemed happy, eager even, to talk about them. Here is Gray as a little boy, she said. And here he is on his first day at school. And this one's at the seaside. My late husband was a keen proponent of photography, she said. And this one – she picked the picture up – is later. She looked at it closely. She handed it to JP. 'My beautiful boy,' she said. 'He loved you dearly JP.' Her hand picked at the lace at her neck. 'I sometimes wonder whether, had he not been taken from us, what might have become of him. Perhaps he was spared the horrors of war, mmm?' She looked at JP. 'But perhaps he might have...' she seemed to be searching for the correct word '... *recovered.*' She meant the drugs.

Did everyone do this around JP? Talk to fill the gaps? She took us cautiously into the later part of her son's life. Leaving school. Struggling to find a position in life that was appropriate for him, and *respectable.* Getting in with the *wrong* people. Sometimes, when she was worried and upset, and even though some of her friends did not approve, she would consult with Mrs Ribble and perhaps – no, *surely* – one day, Gray would talk to her from beyond the grave. She held out that hope, she said, the earnest hope.

She sat up in her chair. 'Are you aware of the dangers of drugs, Mr Baker, of cocaine? You may have read about its effects on some of soldiers? You may have also seen the pamphlets written by my preacher, the Very Rev MacIver?' She rose from her chair and went over to the sideboard where she retrieved some pamphlets and handed them to us. 'For you, JP, and for you Mr Baker. I am also a member of the Christian Association for the Control of Dangerous Drugs. You may have heard of us? You must come to our meetings.' She sat back down. 'I am determined to make some good from what has happened to my son. There was always a risk that Gray would end up … in trouble.'

JP wrote a note and handed it to her. *I wish I could have helped Gray more.*

Mrs R nodded. 'I *know*. Rev MacIver told me that the only answer for Gray was to be born again, that only faith in God could destroy his … addiction.' Her hand went up to the lace at her neck again. 'We told him he must seek help, and forgiveness, and that's when he lost his temper. There was a vase on that table and he picked it up and … smashed it against the wall. I told him he mustn't come back to the house. Not until he was free of … everything.'

'That must have been distressing,' I said.

She nodded. 'Yes, but I didn't keep it up. I was weak. I couldn't live up to my own strictures. A few days later, Gray came to the house and he said he had nowhere to go. So, of course, I allowed him to sleep in his old room. People said at the time I was being too lenient on him, but anything else would have been monstrous. My dear boy would sometimes say to me: 'I still see it mother. I'm standing there with JP and I can see that man stabbing Sarah to death.' It played on his mind. That's where it began, isn't it? It's how the devil got in.'

I could see her eyes filling with tears. She reached down and touched Moll's head. I think it was then I noticed how thin she really was: skin clinging to muscle clinging to bone.

She sat silently for a minute, then looked at JP. 'I don't

know if anyone ever told you exactly what happened … at the end?' JP shook his head. 'Gray was … unable to resist his … addiction at the time and, if you read the pamphlet I gave you, you'll be aware of the pernicious effects that cocaine can have on the mind and the personality. There was a gentleman in one of the houses across the road from where it happened. He saw it. Gray was making his way back to his rooms, God knows where he'd been, probably down to the docks where he knew people who could provide the drugs he sought.'

She put her hand up to her face. 'A terrible place. And my dear boy, insensible to his surroundings, stepped into the street and there was a tram and he was … hit and was killed straight away.'

She grimaced. 'Perhaps he didn't feel pain JP. It was I who had to attend the police station and look at my poor boy and tell them it was him. *Those who sleep in death will also be raised.'* She looked at the pictures on the sideboard, then back at us. 'I protected him as best I could, and I *always* would, but *I wasn't there*. I wasn't there on the street to say: Gray, look out.'

She talked a little bit more about what Gray was like, mostly when he was a little boy, and it felt like she was still looking for the source of the problem, rummaging around in his childhood for clues about how a boy could become a drug addict. Eventually, she seemed to run out of energy and I thanked her for her time – and we left. My last view of her that day was her standing by the door of the house seeing us off, one thin grey hand on the handle of the door, the other raised in a half-wave.

The following day, there was a letter from JP. Tucked into the envelope was a picture. *I thought you might like to see this*. It was a picture of Gray, smartly dressed, and JP, in uniform, and I could see straight away what had happened: JP had signed up on that day in August 1914 and he and his friend had gone to a photographer's studio to capture the moment straight away. Perhaps JP was trying to help his friend; perhaps he thought there was still hope for him, that he could be saved from the drugs. Look at their faces. Gray's looked rather hollow, a bit haunted. JP's was hard to read, but there was some pride in it – knowledge that he'd done the right thing in signing up? But how sad the picture was. JP could not rescue Gray from drugs, or his grief over Sarah Brindle. A few weeks later, he was killed under the wheels of a tram. But look at them, the boys in the picture. Look at JP standing in the light. The light before the dark. And what did I feel? I felt fear. And shame.

8

I don't know exactly why the visit to Mrs R set off some doubts in my mind again, but it did. It also didn't help matters that, as well as the silence I experienced when I was with JP – and I was doing my best to understand it – there were long silences when I wasn't with him. Days and weeks would go by without a letter, or a note, and sitting in my rooms, with only the secrets of the suitcase under my bed for company, thoughts and doubts would nag at me. Was JP … quite well? I also wondered if I was helping him or making things worse. And I was beginning to doubt whether we would ever get to the bottom of who killed Sarah Brindle as long as JP continued with his silence, his refusal to speak.

Eventually, I sat down and wrote JP a letter. I told him how I was feeling about the visit to Mrs R. I said I could see how profoundly she'd been affected by the death of her son and that I'd felt intrusive – impertinent – going to her house and asking her lots of questions. *What was I doing there?* I also told JP that I wondered how we could make any progress. I wanted to be sympathetic. I wanted to be helpful. But I asked him if we could ever get to the truth if we couldn't talk to each other. I also told him about the meeting I'd had with Elizabeth Mackie and a little of what she'd said. I suppose I was hoping he would tell me more. I was also wondering what on earth the next step would be.

I posted the letter the following morning, but almost as soon as I did, I felt some regret. How could I accuse JP of failing to tell me everything when I was sheltering so many secrets myself? I lay on my bed and looked at the cracks on the ceiling. I took the old tag from my pocket and ran my finger over the numbers. 8161. Why did I keep this last remnant of my time in the cells? Was it to remind me that I was right – or wrong? I was a Christian, but I was also a socialist and my conviction, my deepest-held principle, was that the working class of this country have no quarrel with the working class of Germany, or any other country for that matter. And for that principle, I was prepared to go to prison. So why had I not told JP? Maybe it was because, in some place, deeper than my principles, there was a fear that I might be wrong and that I should have been there, with JP, in France. It was the words of my father that hurt the most: *I am ashamed of you.* And he only knew a part of it. He did not know the deeper secret, the deepest one.

JP's reply to my letter came a couple of days later. It was brief but longer than anything he'd written to me before. *'Dear Harry, I wish I could tell you where it started,'* it said. *'I talked at school and I talked in the trenches. I said 'yes sir' a million times, although there wasn't much call to talk in France, only listen. Dig that trench. Dig that grave. And when I saw the horror for myself, I remember deciding I would never speak the truth to my friends at home. And then I decided that I would never speak at all. I do not know why I am like this and I do not know how to make it better but I do hope that one day I will speak again. And when I do, my first words will be to you. I have arranged to see Barbara and Rachel. I hope you will come with me. JP.'*

The letter helped a lot, I have to say, although I realised too that there was so much missing from it. But I couldn't abandon the enterprise now. I was beginning to get a sense that JP was trapped – trapped in his silence – and that perhaps I could help in some way, despite my doubts, and despite my secrets. I thought about our next meeting:

Barbara and Rachel McIntosh. I remembered the classroom photograph and the handwritten names along the bottom.

JP had arranged to meet Barbara first, in the café where she worked. I liked her at once. She was confident with the sort of firm face you remember, framed by dark hair which was cut low over her dark eyes, not very different from the style she wore in the photograph when she was a child. She was still wearing her apron for work when she joined us at the table by the window. The name of the café was over her chest in bid red letters – *High Street Grill.* She smiled at JP.

'So JP,' she said. 'You're still not talking then?' I could see that she didn't mean it vindictively, it was simply the way she spoke: directly.

She looked at me, then looked back at JP. 'So how is this going to work then?' she said. 'You want to talk to me and my sister, but JP doesn't talk.' She sat back in her chair and looked at both of us in turn. 'And what would be the point eh? Of going over it all?' She looked at me. 'Tell me who you are first.' She wiped her hand on her apron.

'I'm a friend of JP's,' I said. I'd hoped that JP would explain all this in his letter to Barbara.

Barbara looked again at JP. 'How long has this been going on now JP eh? Come on, you're an intelligent man. Isn't it time you snapped out of it? We were all affected by what happened to Sarah, but you're *wasting* your life with this … whatever it is.'

I winced slightly as I waited for JP's reaction. In a way, Barbara was saying pretty much what I'd wanted to say to him a few times, but I'd never had the nerve. Barbara did. 'Was it France?' she said. 'I've read about it in the papers. Shell shock. Is that it?' I moved the menus around, for something to do.

'OK,' she said, turning to me. 'JP isn't going to speak. So it's down to us.'

And so we started the same sort-of conversation that JP and I had worked out for each other. I would ask a question. JP would write in his book. And Barbara would fill in the gaps and after a while, after the initial suspicion, or aggression, had faded a little, it seemed like she welcomed the chance to talk about school, and Sarah. I was noticing this more and more with JP: at first, people were suspicious, but then their natural urge to fill the silence took over and they *talked*. For a while, she spoke generally about her school days, and her blossoming friendship with Sarah, and the fun they'd had, but inevitably her thoughts turned to her friend's final day.

'My main memory,' she said, 'is Gray telling me what happened. I was quite close to Gray. He was a lovely boy. You know he was hot on Sarah don't you? I mean, he tried to hide it, but I could see he cared and then he … saw her stabbed to death. It's going to affect you badly that, isn't it? Which it did.'

She pulled the menus towards her and arranged them into a little pile. 'Sarah had boyfriends,' she continued, 'but she was hard-working too at school; boys didn't distract her that much. She wanted to be an actress, and I think she would have been a very successful one too. Her mum and dad weren't over the moon about it, but there you are. When she died, she was preparing for a play. She was good. Talented.'

Barbara took out her purse. 'I've got a picture of Sarah somewhere,' she said. 'I sometimes look at it.' She fumbled around in the purse. 'Here it is.' She took out the small picture and handed it to me and there she was again. Miss Sarah Brindle, actress. The girl who died. Alive again. She was sitting by a small table in the photograph, and leaning forward, her eyes shining under the rim of a hat. There was a little beauty spotted painted on her cheek. JP leaned over and looked at the picture too. It was hard to read his face. But every time I saw a picture of Miss Brindle, I felt something, and it got stronger each time. What was it exactly? A sense of responsibility? Loyalty?

Barbara put the picture back into her purse. Her face was … different, as if something had passed over it then disappeared again, with an effort. 'I liked Sarah a lot,' she said. 'Although I don't think I was quite fashionable enough, you know, to be in her little group. Sarah always had a group of girls around her who were trying to impress her, but I could never be bothered with that, or at least I pretended I could never be bothered. You either like me or you don't. Some don't.'

Barbara put her purse on the table and patted it. 'But the thing about Sarah was that she actually seemed to like everyone. She didn't *judge* them. You know how young girls can be? Judgmental? But she wasn't. She tried to include people. And she knew how to have fun, that's what being an actress was about, I think. Having fun. Even when you're grown-up, or supposed to be.'

JP wrote a note and slid it across the table towards her. *What did Gray tell you about what he saw?* Barbara looked down at the words, then back at JP. 'Do you mean about the day Sarah was killed?' she said. JP nodded. She sat and thought about it. She picked at the edge of the table and started talking, slowly, haltingly, as she recalled what Gray had told her. He'd told her that they'd heard Sarah scream and they'd run up the stairs and they saw the man stabbing Sarah. She paused. Was she upset, or just trying to remember? She continued. The murderer, whoever it was, he was wearing a mask, he slammed the door and Gray tried to kick the door in. And when they got in, Sarah was lying on the floor and the murderer had got out the back window. She finished and looked at JP. 'That's what he told me,' she said.

JP seemed to be considering what she'd said. I looked at him sideways. His pen hovered over his notebook. I suddenly noticed all the sounds in the café. This kept happening in the quiet imposed by JP. He wrote a note and slid it over to Barbara. I could see the words. *I think about that day a lot. But I sometimes think something wasn't there. Did Gray ever say anything like that to you?*

Barbara read the message then put her head to one side as she thought. 'I'm not sure what you mean,' she said. 'Do you mean that there was something missing? Maybe another person, an accomplice or something? Maybe there was more than one that broke in.' She put her head on the other side as she continued to think 'No, I don't think so. Gray never mentioned anything like that.' She picked up her purse and put it back in the pocket of her apron.

She suddenly looked at JP again. 'I mean, you know, don't you, that Sarah was in love with Gray. For a bit. The sort of love you have when you're 18 or 19. But she meant it at the time. You remember, don't you? And I think they walked out together for a while, and then Gray said could they just be friends. And he did it sensitively. And Sarah and he were friends. Gray saw other people and Sarah saw other people and it was fine. There was always a part of Gray that got *bored* of things, don't you think? But that was ages before Sarah died.'

She smiled. A memory had come to mind and it suddenly seemed to lighten the mood. 'Do you remember the time he put a dead mouse in my desk?'

JP smiled. He didn't often smile.

'We were at primary school,' said Barbara, turning to me for a second. 'And I remember opening the lid of the desk and the bloody thing was lying there, dead, with its eyes open and I *screamed* and Gray laughed and the teacher knew straight away it was him even though he denied it. He was always pulling stunts like, practical jokes.' She was smiling again as she stayed in the memory. 'He didn't always know when to stop though. With the jokes, I mean. I don't think they came from cruelty, but I just think he didn't know when to *stop.*'

She paused. 'Can you believe it JP? We're all still so young and Sarah's dead and Gray's dead. Everyone seems to have died. My brother didn't come back from France, did you know that?' She looked out of the window. 'And my cousin. And his father. And every one of the Campbell boys, from down the road. What the hell is going on?' The door opened and some customers came in. Cold air.

'Tell me JP,' she said. 'What are you hoping to achieve with all this? Have you been to the police?'

JP shook his head and started writing again. *I need to find out what happened. Someone tried to push me in front of a car.* He showed the note to Barbara then looked intently at her face for a reaction. Why had he told her? Why now?

Barbara's eyes widened. 'Are you sure? And you think this has something to do with what happened to Sarah?'

Careful slow words on the paper from JP. *It could be the person who killed Sarah.* Cold air again, swirling round our table.

'I don't know what to say,' said Barbara. 'You don't think. I mean, for God's sake, you don't think Gray might have been *killed* do you, deliberately?' She shot a glance at me. 'They said he was …. that he'd taken drugs, but maybe this is what the murderer does – pushes people in front of cars? Dear God.' She ran her hand through her hair.

She looked out of the window again, then back at JP.

'Are you being careful?' she said to him. 'If they've tried to push you in front of a car once, they could try again.' She put her hands up to her face. 'Who is *doing* this JP? Why would they want to kill Sarah and why the hell would they want to come after you? Someone in our class was *mad*. You know that, don't you? *Cuckoo*. We were sitting in that class learning about history and maths and whatever, and someone, in their little brain, was thinking about killing people. I can't bear it.' She stopped and pointed at JP. 'You be careful.' She then turned to me. 'And you look after him. Bloody hell.'

She glanced at her watch and looked at the door. She was a bit shaken. At first, she'd seemed impressive and strong, but how strong was she, really? 'Rachel should be here by now,' she said. She looked at JP again. 'You know, this has upset me JP, it really has. Sarah. Gray. Now you. And you're sitting there *not talking*. We've got to sort this out.' The door opened and Barbara looked up. It was Rachel, her sister.

She came over to the table and said hello and I could see some resemblance to Barbara straight away although the differences were obvious too. Rachel's demeanour was different. Where Barbara was confident and rather loud, Rachel was quieter and more subdued.

She stood around awkwardly for a bit as we shifted around to make space for her and Barbara immediately launched into an explanation of the conversation we'd just had. Rachel seemed shocked, but her reaction was more restrained than her sister's. You felt that, while Barbara put everything on show, Rachel did the opposite and kept it in.

Eventually, Barbara got up and fetched us strong black coffee and said she would leave Rachel and us to talk and

I could see JP leaning in to listen to Rachel, carefully, intently. I got the feeling it was Rachel JP really wanted to hear from. The communication started slowly: written messages and stilted answers, but then, like Barbara, she slowly started to talk about Sarah and the past.

At first, she ran over general memories, of school, and her friends, and Gray and Sarah, and then she asked more about JP's silence. JP answered her questions in short, neat messages, and Rachel nodded, concerned. I could hear Barbara in the background, repeating a customer's order. *Potatoes? Gravy? Something to drink?* Rachel asked lots of questions about JP's time at the Front, and his regiment, and eventually I realised why, when she mentioned Henry. Henry had gone out in the 1914 wave, like JP, and he'd served with the Northumberland Fusiliers too and he'd told Rachel that they would get married when he got back. He never got back.

After a while, JP ripped a fresh sheet off his pad and wrote a question. *I wanted to ask you about the mask.*

Rachel looked at me, like she wasn't sure what the conversation was really about. It was all a coincidence really, she said, that she'd been near the theatre when it happened. She'd stayed late at the library to read, and she was walking home along the street behind the theatre when she heard screams. She would never forget them, she said, but they were *odd*, and she remembers at first that she thought they must be connected with a play. She stopped, she said, and listened, and the screams came another couple of times, and she remembered standing there. Some people say to her: why didn't you run and get help, but she said you're not used to hearing screams and when you do, it stops you.

JP wrote down a question. *And the mask?*

Rachel nodded. 'I was still standing in the street, not sure what to do, when one of the windows was yanked open. I remember the noise of it – the big wooden window being dragged up. And someone threw something out and it fluttered down and it landed close to me.'

'The mask?' I asked.

'Yes. It was a horrible thing. Not like a children's mask at all. I remember the little empty eyes and I picked it up. I know I shouldn't have but I did. It reminds me now, when I think back to it, of the gasmasks you see in the papers. And I looked up at the window and not long after that, I could hear a police car and I ran round to the front of the building.'

I could see that JP hadn't taken his eyes off Rachel. This was important. He scribbled a few words. *Why did they throw the mask out of the window?*

Rachel looked at the note. 'I *know*. I didn't even think it was odd at first. Whoever killed Sarah would want to get rid of the evidence and he'd throw it out of the window, wouldn't he?'

'That's logical,' I said.

Rachel shook her head. 'No, it isn't. I mean, it is *at first* or it feels that way, but this is what I said to the police afterwards when it started to sink in. I've spoken to Babs about it, but she says to drop it, the police would have checked all the evidence. But, well, it was *wrong*.'

'How do you mean, wrong?' I asked.

'Well, the story, or the theory, is that whoever killed Sarah climbed out of a window, and down over the roof of the sheds, yes?' She looked at JP, who nodded.

'Ok,' she went on,' that makes sense in a way, and he must have done that, or *she*, because they escaped somehow. But why get rid of the mask? Why throw it out of the window?'

I shrugged. 'As you say, to get rid of the evidence.'

JP wrote a note and showed it to me and Rachel. *Yes, but why get rid of it then?*

Rachel banged her finger down on the pad. '*Exactly,*' she said. 'Why throw the mask straight out of the window and *then* run away? It would make more sense to keep the mask on and escape with it on, wouldn't it? At least that way, your face would be covered as you're running away because there would be a chance you'd be seen, wouldn't there? But if you throw the mask away and then run away, if someone sees you, they'll see your face and there's more chance you'll be recognised and caught.'

I put a hand up to my face. 'Yes, I *suppose so.* Maybe they panicked.'

Rachel shrugged. 'Possibly,' she said. 'But it irritated me, and I went to the police and they nodded when I told them and they said thank you so much for your time Miss McIntosh, we will consider what you say, but nothing ever came of it. But it bothered me then and it bothers me now.' She turned to JP. 'Is this why you're getting into this all again?'

JP wrote a note. *I want it to make sense.*

Barbara had reappeared by her sister's side. 'How you all getting on?' she said. She started clearing away the cups and there was something about the way she did it that signified the meeting was over. We got up and Barbara shook hands with JP and Rachel did too, a little more shyly, and they said it was nice to meet me, and they wished it had been under better circumstances, and then we were out in the street.

We walked up the road away from the café. JP was barely looking at me. His eyes were fixed on the road ahead and all I could hear were his feet, and mine, on the pavement. Was this an important day? Looking back now and knowing what was about to happen to JP and me, I think it was. I remember thinking about the mask and visualising it twirling and turning in the air as it fell towards Rachel. And there it was: lying there, in the street, its eyes looking up at the sky: dead eyes.

9

I liked Barbara and Rachel a great deal, but I was a little unsettled by our meeting with them at the cafe. Two images kept coming to mind. First, the photograph of Sarah Brindle that Barbara had shown us. I kept seeing Miss Brindle's face in my memory. The head back. The half-smile on her lips. But I also couldn't forget what Rachel told us, about the mask and also the way she described it: black, blank, with gaps for the eyes. I remembered the picture in the newspaper cutting that JP had given me. Those two images together – the young woman smiling, and the mask that covered the face of the man, or the woman, who killed her – they seemed to underline what this whole business was about. And I felt terribly unfit for it, inadequate, useless.

It helped, as it always did, to go out with Corie and for two or three weekends in a row, she and I went out to our favourite dance hall, O'Henri's. Corie admitted she'd developed a terrible crush on the doorman, and I could see what she meant. She said she fully intended to flirt with him and did. Later, we danced and she put her hands round my waist and cocked her head up to me, lips pursed, her eyes heavy with vodka. They were good for me, nights like this.

On other nights, however, I needed to be in a place where Corie couldn't come. When I'd first heard about it, just after the war, I wasn't even sure I believed it existed, but a friend I made in the park gave me the address and told me its name – *The Cave* – and swore me to secrecy but said *you must go*. It took me a while to find the courage though and when I got there, I wasn't sure I'd got the right place. From the front, it looked like an ordinary block of terraced flats. But I knocked on the door and said the password my friend had given me, and I was in and it was … frightening, wonderful, blissful, shameful, heaven. I spoke to Corie about it afterwards, breathlessly, and her eyes widened at the excitement of it. What *would* His Majesty say if he knew! she said. And I thought: what would my family say if they knew? But that first night at The Cave, I made the acquaintance of a beautiful young Welshman with dark curls on his forehead and large, strong hands, and when I told Corie about him she pretended to be scandalised. And the next weekend, I went again and sought out my Welshman and when I couldn't find him, there was someone else. And sometimes I would think: I must tell JP about this place. I hoped he would come. I hoped he would utter the password and step down into all his shocking beauty and *noise*.

I knew the risks of course, and sometimes I would lie in bed worrying about it. I knew that the police might learn of The Cave's existence, or worse: there might be someone eager to make some money. And I also wondered what some of my new friends at the Cave might think if they knew my other secret. *There's only one thing worse than a pansy.* So I'd lie there and promise myself that I wouldn't go back. And the next night, I would.

If I'm honest, my trips to The Cave also helped me take my mind off the dark adventure with JP, but only for so long. I would sit in the library with a book in front of me, reading the same few sentences over and over again, ancient history, and JP and Sarah Brindle and Gray would come to my memory. And, in my mind's eye, I'd see the corridor that led to the place where Miss Brindle died. And there would be an image of JP trying to speak and asking the question *what's at the top of the stairs?* But there was no sound coming out of his mouth. Maybe it wasn't about going to the police, maybe it was about JP going to see a doctor again? Someone who could help him to talk and then, when he could talk … what would he say? *What would I say?*

I think it was the mix of all these emotions that led to what I did next. I was heading up to university one afternoon but instead of going straight on, I took a left into the street that led to the theatre. It didn't look quite so heavy and oppressive this time. I thought about the people who would sit in the stalls and watch thrillers or laugh at comedies. Perhaps they would never be aware of the girl who was stabbed to death at the top of the building. And that made me a little angry. It motivated me: remembrance of Sarah Brindle.

I'd slowed my pace a bit as I was passing the building and was on the point of walking on when I heard a voice behind me.

'You! Are you Harry Baker?' There was an aggressive tone in the voice. The question wasn't friendly.

I turned and coming down the path of one of the little houses opposite the theatre was a man of about my age; short, stocky, red hair. His chin was jutting out towards me and his eyes were dark. I told him, yes, I was Harry Baker. He was close to me now. Too close.

'Why are you going about the place asking questions?' He jabbed a finger at me.

'Questions?' I was spluttering.

'Yes, about what happened at the theatre. To Sarah.'

'I …' He was too close.

'You've been to see Babs and her sister haven't you?' He said. 'Bothering them.'

'We weren't bothering them.'

He put his face even closer to mine. 'Yes, you were.

Rachel's upset, cos of you going about the place like Holmes and Watson. Who the hell do you think you are?'

I took a couple of steps back. Face. Eyes. Jabbing finger. 'I've been helping JP,' I said.

'Yeah, well JP can get lost. We went into all of this when it happened and along you come poncing about and raking it up. Rachel is upset you know.'

'We didn't mean to upset her. *Really.*'

He snarled. Showed his teeth. 'No, I bet you didn't,' he said. 'Rachel has been trying to forget it all and now this.' His hands were formed into fists. Was he going to hit me?

'Who the hell are you anyway?' he said.

'I'm a friend of JP's. He wanted help, and I said I would …' I could feel my heart. Was that my heart?

The man looked back over his shoulder at the house from which he'd emerged. There was someone at the window. I couldn't get a proper look. Was it Rachel? Had she seen me in the street and pointed me out?

'You weren't at school with us, were you?' said the man. 'What the hell has all of this got to do with you?'

'I'm simply trying to help a friend,' I said. The man's fists were tightening, then re-tightening. White skin over knuckles.

'I don't *care* who were trying to help. It took Rachel a long time to recover and I *don't* like seeing her upset.'

I looked at his face, tight, angry, red, and something clicked. *Daniel. Dan.* This was Dan. Older obviously, thinner, but it was the boy who'd been the back of the old picture, behind Gray and Sarah and JP. *Dan.*

'You're Dan aren't you?' My voice sounded a little strangled. There was a flash in my mind. A memory. A memory of a sensation, of the angry face of the chairman of the tribunal. He had red hair too. He had leaned across the table and said to me: *I ask you Mr Baker, what would*

*you do if a German were to rape your sister? What would
you do then?*

Dan had stepped back a little. 'Yes. Dan,' he said. He
jabbed a finger at my chest. 'And it makes me angry to see
Rachel so upset, do you understand?' He narrowed his
eyes.

'I know … we went to the room where it happened.' I
indicated the building behind me.

I could see the anger rising in him again. 'What did you
want to do that for?'

'JP wanted to see where it happened again,' I said. 'You
know how it's affected him… he hasn't talked for a long
time.'

'Yes, I heard. No wonder. All the more reason to *mind
your own business.'*

He looked up at the theatre then back at me. 'Look, I'm
not going to stand round here arguing with you … leave
Rachel alone. And Babs. We do not want to be involved.'
He took his time over every word then turned towards the
house before turning back to me again. 'And by the way,
I'll be telling the police about this.'

He stomped back up the path to his house and shut the
door loudly behind him. And there I was, left standing in
the street, the blood and the adrenaline still gushing
through my body. When I got back to my rooms, I wrote a
quick letter to JP telling him what had happened and
wondering whether Dan might live up to his promise to go
the police. Then I tried to calm myself. I tried to read a
book but the words would not stay in my head. And so I
pulled the suitcase from under the bed and pulled out the
pictures and took comfort in the familiar pleasures.

10

The following morning, I could still feel the effects of the encounter with Daniel and they stayed with me for a while. Pictures kept forming in my mind, particularly last thing at night when everything was extinguished except my ticking brain. The first time I encountered JP. The corridor in the theatre with JP standing in the open doorway. The grieving but somehow rather frightening Mrs R, who loved her son who loved cocaine more. JP walking up the stairs and getting to the top and trying to ask the man without a face who he was. And the mask. *The mask.* Dead eyes; a blank face over-laid on a human one. I could never forget these things. I could never *un-see them.*

And then, about a week later, I received a letter from JP telling me he had been ordered to attend the local police station and the following day I received a similar order. The letter, from a Chief Inspector William Downs, was on the face of it friendly. He informed me he was the officer in charge of the Sarah Brindle affair and he'd like me to attend the Portland Street station, with Mr Allgood, to answer a number of questions in connection with the case. I have to say that, initially, I felt some relief: JP and I really shouldn't have been behaving like amateur detectives and now the police would take over and everything would be fine. But I also knew there was a risk in going there. They might recognise me at the station. They might sneer and say: *nice to see you again Mr Baker.*

An appointment to visit the station was arranged for the following Friday and JP and I met at the end of the street and walked up together. After arriving, we waited at the reception area for about 15 minutes. There was a stone-faced constable sitting at a desk by the door, who paid no attention to us. The door opened. Chief Inspector Downs. Would we come this way please? A vaguely Scottish accent I thought.

We were taken to a small room near the back and directed to sit on one side of the table. Downs took the other side and put a file down on the desk. He was short, stocky, but the face had no fat, only bone and muscle. I supposed he was about 50 years old. He appeared to be relatively friendly. 'Nice to see you again Mr Allgood,' he said to JP. There was a pause. JP didn't say anything. I didn't say anything. Downs didn't say anything. He opened a drawer in the desk and took out a pad and pen which he handed across to JP. 'There has been no change in your condition then I see Mr Allgood?'

Downs sighed heavily and opened the file. 'We have received a complaint that you two gentlemen ...' had he put a little pointed emphasis on the word or did I imagine it? '... have been asking questions of the witnesses to the Sarah Brindle case. Is that true?'

JP pulled the note towards him and wrote slowly and carefully. *I'm entitled to. I was there.*

Downs looked at the pad and I could see his lips tightening. Don't antagonise him, I thought.

He turned to me. 'And what is your connection with the case Mr Baker?'

I shifted in my chair. 'I'm a friend of Mr Allgood.'

'I see,' said Downs. I detected some unspoken emphasis again. He rolled his tongue across his bottom lip. 'You do realise the case is still a matter we are investigating? We are still looking for the man who killed Miss Brindle and it doesn't help having .... *amateurs* on the case if that's what this is.'

I glanced sideways at JP. Was he going to tell him?

About the car? About being pushed in front of the car? I looked straight ahead. The chief inspector was looking at JP closely.

'You know, Mr Allgood, I'm very sad to see that you're still so affected by what happened. Have you had any help since it happened?'

JP wrote a note. *I've consulted doctors.*

'Have they helped?' asked Downs.

JP shook his head.

'I see,' said Downs. He leaned across the desk and knitted his fingers together and that was it: the questions started. What had we done? Who had we seen? What had they said? Why had we done what we'd done? We'll take a break now. Would we like a cup of tea before we continued? It's going to be a long day gentlemen. Did we understand how irresponsible we had been? What was my involvement? How had we met? And there were questions in my head too. Why wasn't JP mentioning the fact that someone had tried to kill him? And why wasn't he mentioning our visit to the theatre? And why was I going along with it? Since when was I a conspirator in the silence?

Eventually, the Chief Inspector seemed to come to the end of his list of questions and shut his file. 'I can't stop you speaking to your friends, gentlemen' … I was right the first time: there was a slightly sarcastic emphasis on that word *gentlemen* … 'But I want you to be very careful. We have not forgotten Miss Brindle. Believe me. We want to find who killed her. But … I insist. Leave it to the professionals.'

He stood up and the meeting was at an end but as JP headed out of the door ahead of me, the Chief Inspector put his hand on my shoulder. 'May I have another minute of your time, Mr Baker?' JP was shown out into reception and I was taken into a side office. The Chief Inspector fixed his eyes on me. He had seen my papers, he said, and his advice to me was to keep out of trouble. Did I think it was wise to involve myself in police matters with *my record*. We do not want amateurs involved in police cases, he said, but we especially don't relish the involvement of a… he leaned across and hissed the final word into my ear … *coward*.

I felt the same way I always did when I was confronted in this way: shame but anger too. I could feel my body trembling. 'Is there anything else Chief Inspector?' I refused to let my voice quaver.

The Chief Inspector shook his head. 'No,' he said. 'There is nothing else that you … *or your type* … can do to help.' He nodded at the door and I hurried towards it. I didn't look at the constable who was sitting by the door and when I reached the street, at first I couldn't see JP. There he was. I took a step towards him. There was no time left for silence anymore, especially from me.

'There's something I must tell you,' I said. 'You're not the only one who's been silent.' I looked back at the police station. 'I've been in prison,' I said. 'While you were in France. When war broke out, I told them straight away that I couldn't fight, that I wouldn't fight and I didn't and I'm not ashamed of it, even though sometimes, when I meet men like you, I am. But I had to tell you in case the police told you.'

I looked at the police station again then back at JP. He had taken his black book out and was writing a note and he showed it to me. Two words. *I knew.*

11

In the couple of weeks that followed the interview with Chief Inspector Downs, our lives resumed relative normality. My intriguing friend behaved as if nothing had changed between us and I was grateful for that, deeply grateful. I knew a little from what Miss Mackie, the nurse, had told me that JP had signed up in August 1914 and that he'd lost friend after friend after friend in the war, so I wouldn't have been surprised if he had rejected me when I revealed to him that I had not fought and, *worse*, that I thought the fighting was wrong. But JP had clearly suspected the truth and it didn't matter. It made me respect, and admire, my silent, frustrating friend a little more.

As for Chief Inspector Downs's warnings, I think I knew straight away that they would not divert us from our course. JP had ignored the fact that someone had tried to push him in front of a car and I had ignored the doubt that was tapping on the inside of my head. And I *was* involved. And even deeper, now that I'd told JP my secret, or one of them at least. So, I suppose both JP and I both thought, separately, the same thing: we've come this far, we keep going.

A couple of weeks after the meeting with Downs, I received a letter from JP in which he told me that Daniel, the red-headed chap who'd accosted me outside the theatre, wanted to meet us. I remembered the man in the street, his face close to mine, eyes wide, teeth clenched, but I agreed, a little reluctantly, that we could meet at the Blue Lamp, the public house near the theatre.

When we arrived a couple of days later, Dan was already at the bar supping at a pint of lager and I could see he was much calmer than he'd been when I'd met him the first time. He ordered us drinks at the bar and we found a table. JP had brought Moll and for a minute of two Dan fussed over her, tickling her ears and putting his face down to hers. This was a different person to the one I'd seen in the street, the angry one.

'Listen,' he said, lighting a cigarette and looking at me. 'I'm sorry about the other day. I lost my temper. Rachel, Miss McIntosh, told me what happened, and I saw red. I'm fond of her and I saw you in the street and I … as I say … please accept my apology.'

I said it was fine.

'I still don't think you should be acting like coppers though,' said Dan. 'And I meant what I said: Rachel was badly affected. We all were.' He looked at JP and for a moment seemed unsure what to say next. 'You're still affected aren't you?'

JP went into his pocket and took out his notebook and started writing. I took a sip of beer and put the glass back down on the table. Clunk. At least it was sound. JP showed Dan his note. *We were all affected, badly.*

Dan looked at the words for a second or two. It turned out that he had been in the same regiment as JP. He mentioned names. He reeled them off. Bought it. Bought it. Bought it. He clasped his hand to his right leg. This is my only wound, he said, I got off lightly. 'I'm all right really,' he said. Then he talked about Gray. 'Gray was a friend of mine too, a *good* friend, and it was upsetting, course it was. I couldn't believe he died like that, hit by a tram.' He smiled wryly. 'At least he died before he could be sent to the trenches with the rest of us eh?'

JP wrote another note. *We went to see Gray's mother.*

Dan took a swig of beer. 'Mrs R? How is she?'

JP wrote quickly. *She'd like to know who killed Sarah. I*

would like to know that too.

Dan drank from his pint again. It was half empty already. A thought flashed across my mind: was this reasonable Dan in the pub the real one, or was it the angry man in the street? There was an edge to him, an *atmosphere* I wasn't sure about yet. I looked at his face, encircled by the smoke from his cigarette.

He took another deep swig of his pint. 'Is Mrs R still ok then?' he asked. 'You know how it upset her. Gray and his … *habits.*' He sighed and shook his head. 'He was such a great kid – I mean, I know he could be troublesome, but he was a great kid. Funny. Really funny.'

JP went into his pocket again and took out the old classroom photograph. Dan's eyes widened as he looked at it.

'My God,' he said. 'Where did you get this?' He picked the picture up and looked at it more closely. 'That's just how I remember us all. Gray.' He pointed at the boy in the middle. 'Look at his face. He always looked a little angry at something didn't he?' He laughed a little. 'And look at me, trying to get attention as usual.'

JP wrote down a question. *Do you remember us all going to a building – maybe a block of flats? A flat at the top of a lot of stairs?*

Dan thought for a minute then shook his head. 'Don't think so.' I thought about the rhyme again. *What's at the top of the stairs, lad? What's at the top of the stairs?*

Dan seemed to be trying to summon up a memory. 'No, I'm sorry, I definitely don't remember any flat when we were kids. Gray lived in a flat, up on Palmerston Hill, later on, when his mother kicked him out, near the cemetery. I went up to see him once. Pretty rough place, but it was all he could afford I think.' He looked at JP. 'Were you still in touch with him at the end?'

JP shook his head.

'No, not a lot of the old gang were. Oh, you should have seen it JP. It broke my heart. The door was open, when I went up to see him, wide open to the street, I remember that, and I thought, why has Gray left his door open and then I went inside and realised; there was nothing anyone would want to steal. There was no furniture, well, virtually nothing. There was an old chair and that was it. And there was nothing in the scullery either. I asked him if he wanted a cup of tea, could I make it, and he said he had nothing and I opened the door to the larder and I … gagged, the smell, there was something in there. I think it had gone off, months before. It was rotten, disgusting. And the shelves were bare. I'll never forget it. All Gray cared about was the … well, you know, the drugs.'

He suddenly changed the subject. 'Do you want another pint? Yes?' He didn't wait for an answer. He attracted the barmaid's attention and ordered three more beers even though JP and I hadn't drunk most of the first one. Moll tipped her head towards the table and licked the dregs of the beer from the bottom of the glasses.

Dan was talking about Gray's flat again. 'I remember, I went into the sitting room, after I'd seen the kitchen and I said to Gray, what's happened mate? what's happened? Why is there no food? Are you not eating? And I could see he wasn't. He was sitting on the chair and he was sunken in. He was so thin. I hadn't seen him for months, I'd avoided him if I'm honest because you have to in the end don't you? He'd borrowed God knows how much money off me, and Rachel, and anyone else who would lend him anything and you get to the end of your tether don't you?'

He pushed his glass round in the puddle of beer that had formed around it. 'I wish I hadn't gone up there really because I could see what the drug had done to him and there wasn't much left. I mean, he was there physically, but it was only a part of him. The other part, the largest part, had been taken by the drugs. And we didn't even talk about Sarah, but that's what it was all about, in the end. He – and you …' He looked at JP '… stood there and watched Sarah stabbed to death and it destroyed you both.' He grimaced slightly. 'No offence JP.'

He picked up the old picture up again and turned it round so we could see the young Gray: round cheeks, shining hair. 'Look at him there,' said Dan. 'A beautiful boy and he messed it up. *No*. The bastard who killed Sarah messed it up for him.'

'Was Gray getting help?' I asked. 'When you saw him, I mean? His church maybe?'

Dan shook his head. 'He said he was. He was trying to give the drugs up, but I knew he was lying. It was obvious, although God knows where he was getting the money. Thieving, I suppose. It was scary, seeing him in that state. I mean, I knew the drugs were bad for him, but that was ….'

He put the picture down. The barmaid had arrived with three pints on a tray. Dan looked deep into his glass for a while.

'I gave him some money that day,' he said, as if he was answering a question we hadn't asked. 'It wasn't a lot, and I shouldn't have done it. It was the picture of Sarah that did it. It was about the only thing he had in that flat,' he said, 'that picture, and I didn't notice it 'til later on. It was sitting on the floor by the side of the chair on top of a pile of papers. I'd given him the money and he kept saying thanks and he would pay me back, and I said it's fine and he leaned over the chair and picked up the picture of Sarah and he burst into tears. I'd never seen Gray cry before. He said 'this is what it's all about, this is why I'm here'. It broke my heart.'

Dan picked up his pint and took a deep swig. 'Gray said he'd never recovered from Sarah dying. He ended up where he ended up and ...' He stopped and looked down at Moll.

JP waited for a minute or two then wrote a few words. *Did Gray say anything about who killed Sarah?*

Dan looked at the note and shook his head. 'No, nothing.' He looked intently at JP. 'I mean, you were there, we were fairly ordinary kids weren't we? There were rivalries but that's normal isn't it?'

JP wrote again. *Barbara said one of us was mad.*

Dan read what JP had written and put his head over the back of the chair and looked at the ceiling. His head dropped forward again. 'She could be right, couldn't she? Barbara. Unless it was a stranger. You know, someone from outside who broke into the theatre.'

He turned his glass of beer round several times. 'I have sometimes wondered if whoever killed Sarah was part of the problem for Gray. You know, the fact that no one was ever found. The fact that he saw the killer do it, in front of him, and yet he never discovered who it was. Sarah and he were good friends, and they went out a few times. Then he stopped it. But there were no hard feelings and they were still close and that's crossed my mind: maybe he saw something, or knew something, and it bothered him and the only way to cope was ... the way he coped.'

'Yes, but couldn't he have just gone to the police?' I asked.

Dan shrugged. 'Maybe the 'someone' was someone he didn't want to report to the police. A friend, I don't know. I wish I'd asked Gray if he knew who killed Sarah. I don't know if he did, but I sometimes *wonder*.'

He looked down at the picture again and smiled. 'He was

a good looking boy, wasn't he? Gray. No wonder Sarah fell for him.'

'And there were no hard feelings?' I said. 'When he put an end to it?'

'No, but I think that's why Sarah dying upset him so badly, because not only did he see the murder, I think he still loved her a bit, as a friend. That's what it's like when you're young, isn't it? It's intense at that age and to see her die, well, it was the start of the way down wasn't it?'

He talked for a little while longer and asked for my address in case he should need to get in touch. And he talked a bit more about Gray and how, when they were younger, they'd go behind the sheds for a fag and then suck on sweets to hide the smell before they went back into class. And, as he spoke, I realised I quite liked him and a thought sprang to mind: *he's easier than JP.* And another thought: Dan was just another of the children in that photograph. And one of them died and the rest of them were broken. Dan, and his anger. Gray, and his drugs. JP, and his silence.

12

Dan stayed on my mind for days after we saw him, or rather his description of Gray did. Every time I thought about Gray, I could see the blond boy in the photograph and I could see the man he'd become, the man Dan described: thin, starved, hungry for the drug on which he'd become dependent. Why had it happened to him? Perhaps it was some inherent weakness, a frailty of personality, or the horror of seeing his friend Sarah Brindle killed in front of him. I also thought of his poor mother, Mrs R, praying for hope while he was alive, and talking to spiritualists after he had died.

And what of the effects on JP? He witnessed the same terrible event and if JP were – I am reluctant to use the word – *normal*, he would have talked about it. I would have asked him what happened, and he would have told me. Instead, I had bits and pieces written on paper and in letters. And it struck me then: I don't even know what JP sounds like. *I've never heard his voice.*

The interview with Chief Inspector Downs was also playing on my mind. I kept remembering his unpleasant, pale face as he told us not to get involved and I could still summon up the smell of his breath as he leaned towards me and hissed that word: *coward*. Other questions were bothering me too. Why had JP not told the Chief Inspector about being pushed under the car? And why had I remained silent? Perhaps it was because I recognised the chief inspector as the type of man I had encountered over and over again during the war. To people like Chief Inspector Downs, I am the worst of the worst. They have special words for me, and I have heard them a thousand times. *Conchie. Pansy.*

And so, while I waited for JP to get in touch again, I resumed my normal life, such as it was. Corie and I went to O'Henri's a few times and I allowed myself to confess some of my concerns to her, and Corie smiled, leaned across the table, and told me the police could *go to hell*, although Corie never give me all the comfort I needed. Later, I took the long way back to my rooms, past the park, and slipped into the familiar pattern. At first, there was no one around but then I spotted someone: dark, early 20s. *Do you have a light?* He reminded me of one of the dark men in the pictures under my bed. We walked into the park, and while we were there, it didn't matter, all the worries I had about JP, and the police, and the murder we'd somehow ended up investigating. And Corie was right: the police could *go to hell.*

The following morning, there was a message from JP. He said he'd found a photograph. He believed it was significant and he'd like to know where it was taken and thought Mrs R might be able to help. Would I come with him to see her again? An appointment was duly arranged and we met near Mrs R's house. JP had Moll the dog with him. He went into one of the deep pockets of his coat and took out the photograph he'd mentioned. There were three children in the picture whom I recognised at once as Sarah Brindle, Gray and JP. They were perhaps 11 or 12-years-old and they were arranged at the bottom of a staircase. On the left of the picture, sitting on the third step, was the young Sarah, hands in her lap. In front of her, sitting on the second step, was JP, who was leaning back against the banister looking intently at Sarah. And behind them both, standing, was Gray, his face turned down, his head bright in the light from the window. The picture had obviously been taken in a tenement of some kind, but I wasn't sure why it mattered so much to the mystery we were trying to solve.

JP put the picture back in his pocket and we walked towards Mrs R's house. There was a slight drizzle now and every now and again Moll would shake the rainwater off her back. Occasionally, I noticed JP putting his hand down towards her and stroking her neck or tousling her ears and I could see, not for the first time, that my friend could communicate with his dog (and she with him) in a way he couldn't with people. In one of his letters, many months later, he told me that his regiment had once adopted a mongrel as their mascot and that she'd stayed with them in the trenches for many months. She'd been wounded, and gassed, and buried by shellfire, but survived it all. JP promised himself: when I get back to Blighty, I shall have a dog of my own.

Mrs R seemed pleased to see us. She served tea from a silver pot and fussed over Moll and pressed biscuits and cake on us, and eventually JP showed her the picture. She put her glasses on the end of her nose and peered at it. 'My beautiful boy,' she said. She took a second or two to gather her emotions. She looked at JP. 'Is this yours?'

I leaned forward in my chair. 'We wondered if perhaps you knew where the picture was taken,' I said.

Mrs R looked at the photograph again. She narrowed her eyes. 'No, I don't think so. A friend's house maybe? You don't remember?' She turned to JP. He shook his head.

Mrs R held the picture more closely to her face. 'It could be anywhere couldn't it, but I'm sorry. I don't know. Is it important?'

I looked at JP. Why was I hearing the little rhyme in my head? Why was it always the rhyme? *What's at the top of the stairs, lad? What's at the top of the stairs?* Mrs R was looking at the pictures from the sideboard. 'I probably shouldn't have so many photographs here,' she said. 'They are a reminder of … I must remember that my son did *not* die and that he lives on … with Christ.' I remembered the words from Corinthians she'd quoted to us: *Those who sleep in death will be raised.*

She patted her skirts down with those thin pale hands. We sat and drank tea and listened to her remembrances. Gray had been a charming boy, she said, a beautiful soul, and she felt sure that, had he lived, he would have made a fine officer. He would have served his King and done his duty, she said. And I thought to myself: *no, he would have died in the mud.* The clock chimed. Moll lifted her head. Someone walked past outside.

I was just about to make an excuse to leave when Mrs R leaned forward and fixed us with an intense expression. 'I have never told you this,' she said, 'but I did tell the police, Chief Inspector Downs – *not a nice man* – and nothing was ever done. Before Gray died, before he was hit by the tram, he told me someone was following him. At first, I thought it was just the effect of his … addictions. But I came to believe that it was true. I'm sad to say that he owed quite a lot of money to people towards the end, dangerous people.'

She looked past us at the window. 'He was frightened and said someone was trying to kill him. He said they'd killed Sarah and now they were coming for him and he was *frightened.*' A hand went up to the lace round her neck. 'And when he passed away, when he fell under that tram, I said to the Chief Inspector: 'someone was trying to kill my son, someone *pushed* him under that tram.' But they wouldn't believe me and I believe it was because they dismissed Gray as … a criminal.'

I looked at JP. He took his notebook out and wrote a message slowly and carefully. I could see the words from where I was sitting. He passed the book to Mrs R. *I think someone tried to push me under a car.*

Mrs R put on her glasses again and read the words, her eyes widening. 'Is this true?'

JP nodded.

Mrs R read the words again and shook her head. 'God help us.' she said. Her hand reached out to the bible on the table. 'We must *catch* this person.' She sat up straight. 'Have you gone to the police JP? Have you spoken to the Chief Inspector?'

JP nodded again. A silent lie.

'I was right, wasn't I?' said Mrs R. 'Someone tried to push you in front of a car and for all we know they did the same to Gray, my dear, precious Gray. Someone pushed him in front of that tram as well. I *know it.'* Her hands dropped down into her lap. 'I will never forget the day I had to visit the police station and the constable showed me to a terrible, cold, grey room and I could see that the body lying on the table was my dear boy. His face was so white, *so pale.'*

JP leaned forward and put his hand on Mrs R's knee. It was quite unlike him, reaching out like that. Mrs R put her hand on top of his. 'It's not something I ever should have had to do,' she said.

We continued to sit with Mrs R for some time as she talked over other more pleasant memories of Gray. She said her work with the Christian Association for the Control of Dangerous Drugs was a great comfort to her and that it was a way of encouraging some good from the bad of her son's death. She said we must take some of the association's pamphlets and I said I'd be delighted to and she talked a little more about Gray. Towards the end of our visit, JP showed her the picture of Gray and JP and Sarah on the stairs again, just in case. But her answer was the same: she didn't know where it had been taken. And with that, she told us we must come again and showed us out.

We were just about to leave by the front gate when I heard Mrs R's voice.

'Oh Mr Baker!' She was calling from the front door. 'You forgot the pamphlets. From the association?' I told JP to wait for me and headed back up the path.

Mrs R ushered me inside. 'Come in, come in,' she said and as soon as I stepped inside the hall, she grasped me by the arm and put her face close to mine. I could see the lines at the side of eyes. 'I wanted to take this opportunity Mr Baker,' she said. Her voice was rushed, anxious. 'I do hope you know what you're doing.' Her hand tightened on my arm. 'We do *worry* about JP sometimes,' she said. 'I wanted to tell you to be careful.'

'I'm not sure I know you mean,' I said. But I had a memory of Elizabeth Mackie, the nurse, saying something similar.

Mrs R released her grip on me a little. 'Poor JP has been badly damaged by the war,' she said, 'but I think, perhaps, that some of the damage was there *already*. His family was unusual Mr Baker. Some would say I indulged Gray, spoiled him even, but I think JP's problem was the opposite.' She straightened her back and shook her head. '*Oh that man*,' she said. 'I remember JP, when he was really quite young, he would come here and we would give him and Gray milk and cake and I got the impression that he felt a little more able to be himself here. Away from his father.'

I glanced through the open door. JP was still standing at the gate. Mrs R was still holding on to my arm. 'I remember once,' she said, 'poor JP telling us, as we sat round the table in the kitchen, that his father had *beaten* him terribly and that his mother came between them, to stop it.' She shook her head. 'Terrible. I believe in discipline Mr Baker, but I think perhaps JP's father thought he could beat his son into submission or into being the boy he wanted him to be. And I remember little JP sitting at the table and talking about his father and saying that one day he would never speak to him again.' She released her grip. 'You see what I mean? *Never speak to him again.*' She leaned in close again. 'I was always worried about the boy, long before the war. And I worry about him even more now. He's been hurt. And you must be careful.'

She suddenly relaxed her grip. 'But JP is waiting,' she said, 'and you wanted those pamphlets.' She went to a drawer in a cabinet behind the door and took out three or four colourful booklets and thrust them into my hand. 'There you are,' she said. 'I do hope you'll see how valuable our work is at the association, and perhaps even consider joining us.' She guided me to the door and held it open for me. I thanked her for the pamphlets and headed down the path towards JP and Moll.

13

I didn't breathe a word to JP about what Mrs R said to me but I did promise myself I would keep an even closer and more careful watch on JP as well as do what I could to help him. And so I wrote to JP and, in the most discreet way possible, told them there were places one could go. I did not mention The Cave by name – it would have been reckless to do so in case my letter fell into the wrong hands – but if JP's unhappiness was caused by more than the war, if it ran deeper than that, then, with that at least, I could help. I posted the letter the following morning.

When the reply came, there was no mention of my reference to The Cave. Instead, JP's attention was still fixed on the old picture – the one of him, Gray and Sarah on the stairs – and finding the place where the photograph was taken. He wanted to go up to the apartments near the graveyard, near where he grew up, and look around and try to find the building in the picture and he asked me if I would go with him. *I have an idea that it will help*, he wrote. *Maybe if I find that place, the memories will come.* I sent a reply agreeing to the plan, but some of what Mrs R told me kept coming back to mind. I could see her face as she leaned towards me, her hand tightening on my arm, and told me that JP was fragile. I had to be careful, cautious, for JP's sake and my own.

I met JP the following week. We met by the church gates and Moll was with him and I made a fuss of her and we started trudging through the graveyard towards the two apartment buildings at the top of the hill. JP let Moll off the leash and she hurried ahead, stopping to sniff this and that. The wind lifted the ends of JP's coat and he had to put his hand up to stop hair getting in his eyes. I read some of the gravestones as we passed them. *1884, aged 23. 1907, aged 3.* I thought, inevitably, of all the dead who weren't buried here. The men out in France. I didn't say anything. I was more used to our silent relationship now.

About halfway up the hill, JP turned to his right and started following a path that ran along the side of the hill. A row of oak trees cast deep shadows over us. The gravestones here were cleaner, there were more flowers, the people here had died more recently and there were still people alive to tend to their remains. Eventually, they would stop coming as well.

JP stopped by one of the stones. I moved up next to him and read the inscription and realised, with a start, what it was. It was Gray. This was where Gray was buried. *Beloved son who parted this life September 16th, 1914, aged 21. Though worms destroy this body yet in my flesh shall I see God.* Clean white letters against black marble. There were fresh flowers too. I remembered something I'd never seen: Mrs R, Gray's mother, bending down and putting them there.

I'm not sure how long we stood there, still, quiet – it was a long time – but by a graveside, silence is … appropriate. I looked back down the hill at the park and beyond the river. 'It's a beautiful spot,' I said.

I looked at JP. Why had he wanted to come here? I moved closer to the gravestone. 'Fresh flowers,' I said, for something to say. 'Mrs R presumably.' I leaned down and cupped some of the flowers in my hand. I suddenly remembered their name. *Anemones.*

It took us another few minutes to reach the top of the hill and JP seemed even more uncommunicative than ever by the time we reached the top. It's unexpected: for a man who doesn't speak, JP has a way of going into an even deeper silence. He kept his hands thrust into the pockets of his coat, his eyes on the hill up ahead. The apartment buildings at the top were ugly things: cold sandstone, stained with rain, and wind, and bird dirt. I looked back the way we'd come. The gravestones stood in ranks.

JP stopped and looked up at the flats then headed inside and started for the stairs, taking them two at a time, Moll just behind him. On the first landing, he stopped and looked around. I remembered the picture of JP, Gray and Sarah Brindle. This *could* be the place. Possibly. JP took the picture out of his pocket. He looked at it, then looked around at the landing and the stairway, comparing the two. He put the picture back in his pocket, then headed up the stairs to the next landing. There were five flights of steps in all and JP took them quickly. At the top was another landing and double doors that led to a flat, featureless roof. JP went outside and moved to the edge of the waist-high wall that circled the roof and looked down over the hill.

I went over and stood beside him. It was exposed up here. Windy. Cold. The breeze caught Moll's long ears and blew them in front of her face. I was standing to JP's right and noticed the scar under his jaw that ran down his neck and disappeared into his collar. It was, I thought, the only physical evidence of his time at the front, that red line on his white skin. Then I remembered all the times his hand had trembled. Not for the first time, I wondered what he'd seen in France. What had he done? What had been done to him?

'This couldn't be the place?' I said. In the distance, a chimney churned out smoke.

JP kept looking out, reading the sky, and, from nowhere, I had that feeling again, that he might suddenly turn to me and say something. He hand had gone up to his collar and he was pressing his thumb and forefinger against his jaw. I noticed the scar again; it seemed a little redder. Could he force the words out? Could he massage them up and out of his mouth? No. Nothing.

He took out his notebook and wrote, the wind catching the pages. *I wish I could remember where it was. This is all about memory. It's about what I can't remember...* He had underlined the last sentence. The wind caught the page again and turned it over. He held it down, then closed the notebook and headed for the door, I followed him, my feet loud on the stairs.

I didn't say anything on the way back down the hill. JP and I parted company back down by the church and, as I walked home, I began to pine a little for normality, for the simple pleasures of a conversation. Perhaps Corie would like to go out and we would sit and listen to the music and people *talking*. Or perhaps I would go to The Cave and lean into the door and whisper the password. Or perhaps I would go to the park again, if no one was watching, and I could be normal with someone I didn't know.

By the time I finally reached my rooms, it was almost dark, and rather cold, and as usual, the key to my room was sticky. I pushed the door open and it disturbed something on the floor. Two or three letters. I picked them up and put them on my desk. I slipped my jacket off and put it over the chair. I put the kettle on the little stove, turned it on, and went back to the mail. The top letter, I noticed, didn't have a stamp. I wondered if it might be from JP. But then I thought: no, it couldn't be. I'd only just left him.

I opened the letter. There was a single sheet inside, folded over. I unfolded it and read it. I could feel my brain shifting, jolting even, as if it had suddenly lost its balance. A ship. Listing. Sinking.

The note said, in large capital letters: *WE KILLED SARAH BRINDLE AND WE WILL KILL YOU TOO.*

14

As soon as I read the words, scrawled across the page in threatening capitals, I went to the other rooms on the landing and asked my neighbours if they'd seen anything or anyone. Will Pickering, who lives in the flat by the stairs, stuck out his bottom lip and shook his head. He hadn't seen anything, *sorry*. Peter Staines said he'd been out most of the day. I checked with Mr Johns, the caretaker, but he said the same: *nothing*. There are people coming in and out of the building all the time – whoever left the letter wouldn't even have needed a key. They could have just followed someone into the building.

I looked at the words again. *WE KILLED SARAH BRINDLE AND WE WILL KILL YOU TOO.* The handwriting looked normal, a little old-fashioned maybe – that swoop of the S in Sarah – but perhaps whoever wrote it would have disguised their handwriting. Isn't that what you would do? And why those words? *WE KILLED SARAH BRINDLE AND WE WILL KILL YOU TOO.* Why *'we'?* Was more than one person involved in all of this? I read it again, walking the length of my sitting room. The kettle was rattling on the stove. I'd forgotten about it. I switched it off. I imagined someone coming up the stairs and sliding the envelope under my door and I could feel something I'd never really felt before in all the time I'd known JP, not really. *I was frightened.*

I went out into the hall, looked up the telephone number of the police station and called them from the device in the hall. I told them my name and asked if I could see an officer in an important matter. Yes, Chief Inspector Downs was available. Was there anyone else? No, I'm afraid not sir. When could I come into the station? He could see me tomorrow, at 10.30. I said ok, rang off, sat down and wrote JP a letter to tell him what had happened.

I lay on my bed and tried to get to sleep. It didn't come. There were phrases and words in my head. *Something wasn't there. Memory. Memory.* I turned over and faced the wall. *We will kill you too. You too.* And the nursery rhyme. Always that bloody nursery rhyme. Why do we sing that kind of stuff to children anyway? *I took him by the left leg and threw him down the stairs. Here comes a chopper to chop off your head. It's the man without a face.* A memory of my teacher and I. A long time ago. I ask her: *Miss, why did the blackbird peck off the maid's nose?* I turned over again. *Blackbird. Blackbird. Chop off your head.* I must have fallen asleep eventually.

The next morning, I headed to the police station and was led by an uninterested young constable to the same room where Chief Inspector Downs had interviewed JP and I a few weeks before.

'Nice to see you again Mr Baker. Take a seat.' The scrape of wooden chair legs on a wooden floor. There was no indication of that sneer that had been on his face. But the politeness was too studied to be genuine.

I told him what had happened. I took the letter out of my pocket and put it on the table. The Chief Inspector peered at it without touching it. His eyes narrowed. 'Do you have any idea who might have sent this?' he said.

'Well, it's obviously the same person who killed Sarah Brindle isn't it?' *And the same person who pushed Gray under the tram and JP under the car.* But I didn't say anything about that. Still loyal. *Loyal and stupid.*

The Chief Inspector opened his notebook and started asking questions, in the same quick way he'd done before. Where had I been on the day I'd received the letter? Did I notice anything different about my room, or the hallway, or the landing? Did I have anyone in my life who might send such a thing, even as a joke? Was there someone who didn't like me? He also gave me his warning again, in several different ways, about getting involved in a serious police matter. The message was clear: *you have put yourself in danger Mr Baker.* He told me that he would keep the letter and the envelope in the meantime to examine it closely and told me he would be in touch in due course. I wouldn't hold my breath.

I walked away from the station, in a black mood suddenly. I knew JP and Gray had witnessed a terrible event – they'd seen their friend murdered in front of them. They were victims. But I also thought about the person who'd written that letter and crept up the stairs of my apartment and was apparently prepared to kill again. Why was JP so calm? Why wasn't he weeping and wailing? That's what you're supposed to do. You don't simply … stop talking. And you shouldn't expect the people around you to act like it's normal either. But that's what we were doing. That's what *I* was doing. And now it was putting me in danger. Then I felt a stab of guilt: JP went to France. He was in actual danger.

Knock. Knock. Someone was rapping on a window. I hadn't noticed that I was walking by the café. *Knock. Knock.* It was Barbara. She was knocking on the window from the other side, beckoning me in. I hesitated for a second. I was still in a peculiar mood. Barbara came to the door and opened it. 'Hello again,' she said. 'How are you?' I smiled wanly and said fine, yes. 'Coffee?' she said, stepping back. 'You look rather cold.' I didn't move. 'Come on. On the house.'

It was warm in the café, and comforting. I could feel the edges of my mood softening. Barbara showed me to the seat by the window and went to make the coffee. I watched her get a cup and saucer and adjust the machine and for a moment her face was surrounded by the steam. She looked normal. I needed normal. She came over and put the coffee down in front of me then plonked herself down in the seat opposite me.

'How are you?' she said.

I shrugged. 'Fine. It's nice to see you again.'

Barbara smiled. 'You too. I've been thinking about you since the last time we met.'

'Really?' I picked up my coffee. Too hot.

'Yes, well, I was worried I was a bit *rude*, you know. And I was worried about you and JP.' She put the dishcloth she'd been holding down on the table in front of us and patted it down. 'JP is *difficult* and I thought you'd maybe become his … hostage.'

'Hostage?'

She screwed up her face. 'Maybe hostage is the wrong word. But all the talk about helping him to find out who killed Sarah. I wasn't sure what to make of it, or how you'd got involved, or *why* you were involved. I mean, what are you? His assistant? His translator? What?'

'I'm just helping him as a friend.' *I wasn't sure today why I was helping him.*

Barbara patted the dishcloth again. 'Okay … but you need to be careful.' Should I tell her about the letter pushed under my door? I sipped my coffee.

Barbara leaned across the table. 'I'm worried about JP as well,' she said. 'But he upsets me a little too. All the *silence*, the not talking, I don't have a lot of sympathy for it. I mean, I *do* have sympathy for JP. He saw Sarah being killed for Christ's sake. In front of him. So did Gray. It's just that I don't have much sympathy for all the … wallowing.' She grimaced. 'I'm not choosing my words very well today.'

I shook my head. 'No … not at all … the way JP has reacted is …. hard to understand sometimes.'

Barbara smiled. 'He always was a little eccentric. Even at school. *Especially* at school.' She folded her cloth. 'He always had his nose in a book. And he didn't say much, even then.' She looked out of the window. A customer was consulting the menu that was taped to the glass. 'Maybe we shouldn't be surprised,' said Barbara. 'JP never did say very much so eventually he just … stopped talking altogether.'

I thought of the picture of JP with Sarah and Gray on the stairs again. 'Being friends with Gray and Sarah must've helped?' I said.

'They were quite a little gang by the end,' she said. 'But JP was bullied a bit I think. But he was funny, and quick-witted and that protected him from the worst of it. And I think, because he was *sensitive*, there was a bit of name-calling as well … God knows how he managed at the Front. Made a man of him I suppose … or destroyed him.'

'And the murder? Sarah's death?' I said.

'He still hasn't come out of it has he? And he's going to have to some day or he'll ... go mad. You've *got* to talk to people haven't you? *Talking keeps you sane.'* She sat back in her chair. 'Do you want anything to eat by the way? A bacon sandwich? Toastie?' I said I should be heading off. Finish your coffee, she said. She started asking questions about me. Where I was from, where I grew up, how I met JP, university. And as usual, I started to feel tense, like I always did when people asked me questions because I thought: it's only a matter of time before they ask me *the* question: what did you do in the war? And so I changed the subject and bits and pieces emerged about Barbara too. She was close to her sister. She worried about her. And all

I could think was: were you there? Were you there when something happened to an ordinary group of children at a school that ended in one of them dying? Were you there when the seed was planted?

I realised suddenly that Barbara was saying something about her time at school, something about a play. '... and we were backstage. Me. JP. And a few others. A rehearsal, I think. And JP said something, I don't remember what it was and one of the other boys said 'you shouldn't act like that, that's why people say the things they do about you' and I remember the look on JP's face. He kind of shrivelled up and didn't say anything.' She fiddled with the dishcloth. 'I sometimes wonder if ... well, if JP, when he was young, he ... well ... learned not to speak about certain things.'

The door to the café opened and an old couple who'd been looking at the menu came in and Barbara showed them to a table. I got up and straightened my jacket and went to the door. Barbara came over again. 'It was lovely to see you again,' she said. She patted me on the shoulder. 'Take care and pop in for a chat again ... if you need to.'

I thanked her – I meant it – and she went back behind the counter. I went out into the street and paused for a minute. I had no idea where to go. Or who to speak to. I started walking up towards my rooms and a sentence followed me, from the café, something Barbara had said, right at the end: *JP learned not to speak.*

15

My mood was unsettled in the days following the meeting with Chief Inspector Downs. The threat of the letter kept nagging at me – *we killed Sarah Brindle and we will kill you too* – and it didn't help when the Chief Inspector wrote to me a week or so later to tell me there were no immediate leads in the case. JP wasn't much use either. He wrote to me to say he understood why I had gone to the police but didn't think it would get us very far. And, in a way, I understood what he meant. After Sarah's death, he'd been surrounded by police, and doctors and none of it had helped him, not really. He still didn't know who killed his friend. But there was something about JP's attitude that frustrated me a little too. Someone had tried to push him under a car for Christ's sake and now someone – the same person probably – was threatening me. It was unsettling, frightening, and JP was acting like we could resolve it ourselves. In fact, I didn't really know what JP was thinking because he would never tell me. He would never speak. I kept my distance from him for a while. *I could be silent too.*

It also helped, as it almost always did, to get back to the land of the talking with other people. Corie and I went out a couple of times and there were a few moments when I thought I'd tell her about the letter and the visit to the police and all the rest of it. But Corie chattered on and talked about a chap she'd been seeing and, as she shouted over the music about what an unreasonable bastard he was being, I thought: this is what I need, this is good: *talk*. And the second time we went out, I was at the bar ordering drinks when a chap I vaguely knew from university, Jamie, a music student, trombonist, talked to me and we went back to his rooms and the next morning, I thought: it doesn't matter if this night with Jamie is a single event, it's just what I needed after the last few weeks with JP.

Sometimes, I'd feel guilty – guilty for judging JP by the usual conventional rules and the ordinary patterns of behaviour. I wanted to help him. I wanted to help him find out who killed Sarah. Sometimes, I would sit up in bed and run it over in my mind. JP and Gray standing in the corridor looking at *someone* standing over Sarah with a knife. The killer slamming the door and locking it. Gray trying to kick the door down and screaming Sarah's name. JP running down the stairs to get help. The police arriving, breaking down the door. Sarah Brindle on the floor. And I would keep the light on and try to get some sleep.

What wakened me sometimes was the thought of the warning that had been pushed under my door. *WE KILLED SARAH BRINDLE AND WE WILL KILL YOU TOO.* I'd lie there and imagine someone approaching my rooms and standing outside the door. Did they put their ear to the door to check if I was inside? Had they been watching my rooms beforehand? Would they come back? Some nights, I'd listen for sounds from the corridor outside. A door opening. Closing. A voice. Loud at first. Then quieter. Quieter. Gone.

Occasionally, I would receive a note from JP. He was revisiting some of the places from his childhood, he said, looking for the building in the photograph. And then finally, about three or four weeks after we'd visited Elizabeth Mackie at the hospital, I got a note from him saying he'd made a breakthrough. *I think I may have found the building in the picture. Will you come with me? Meet you at the bus station on Driver's Lane, tomorrow, 2pm. JP*

The next day I was there at 2pm sharp and we got on the bus that headed out of town. Moll was with him and went to sleep by our feet. The bus took us out by the main road and up the hill into the north of the city. On one side of the road was a shabby church; on the other, some grotty shops; and straight ahead some new houses. The bus rumbled up the hill. I sat in silence. JP barely looked away from the window.

After about 15 minutes, he tugged at my sleeve and signalled for me to get up. We got off the bus. Behind us the city was laid out in grey. JP pointed ahead to a path that led away from the bus stop. It weaved through some trees and past a scrubby bit of woodland where people had been dumping rubbish, bits of wood and rubble.

'Do you remember being here?' I asked.

JP shrugged. The gravel crunched under our feet. After a few minutes, we reached a clearing in the trees and ahead of us was a block of flats.

JP tried the main door. It was open. Beyond it was a small foyer with a lift and a booth, presumably for the nightwatchman, but it was all locked up and there was no one there. We hung around for a few seconds, then JP headed for the stairs. I could feel a new determination in him, like he knew his destination. I followed. One flight of steps. Another. Inevitably, I heard those words again. *What's at the top of the stairs, lad? What's at the top of the stairs?*

We came to the first landing. There were three doors. Flat 1A, 1B, 1C. There was a faint smell of disinfectant. Above us, on the floor above, a dog barked and Moll cocked her head to one side. JP stopped and took the photograph out of his pocket. He held it up, then stood back, comparing it with the hallway we were standing in. I went over and looked. There it was: the banister, the turn in the stairs, the decorated tiles, and the window up above. It was the same place. We were here.

We took the stairs to the next landing. Then the next. At one point, a couple of young boys came out of one of the flats. They looked up shyly but JP didn't even glance at them. Up again. Third floor. Fourth. JP was speeding up. I was losing my breath a bit. JP didn't seem out of breath at all.

On the fifth floor he stopped and went to the window on the landing. I went and stood beside him. Up here, you could feel the wind rattling the window frame. JP's face was pale, drawn, intense. He looked at me then headed for the stairs again. Up. He was taking the steps two at a time. Seventh floor. We were at the top. There was nowhere else to go.

There were three flats up here, on the top landing. 7A. 7B. 7C. The door furthest away from us, 7C, was open. I could see a small hallway beyond the open door. Faded brown carpet. Pale wallpaper. I looked at JP but he didn't look at me. He took a few steps forward then stopped. I thought: don't hesitate now. He took another few steps towards the door and I followed. We stepped into the hall. Narrow. JP in front. Me behind. Moll behind me. Glimpse of a kitchen to the right. A bedroom to the left. End of the hall. Living room. Window. Light pouring in. A man was standing by the window. He had his back to us. I thought: *what's at the top of the stairs?* How long did the three of us stand there? I wish I could remember. But it was the man by the window who moved first. He turned round. At first, in the bright light, I couldn't make out his face; it was dark, shadowed. *The man without a face.* Then my eyes adjusted. I could see him now. I knew the face. It was different, changed, but I knew it. I'd seen it in photographs a hundred times.

It was the boy who died.
It was Gray.
It was Gray.
It was Gray.

16

Do not ask me exactly what happened next because I cannot remember all the details. I know JP made the first sound I had ever heard him make and I know it was a sound I'd never heard anyone make before. It was a deep, dark cry of pain, shock, anguish – all of those things – and it came in a long painful howl when he realised who he was looking at, when he realised who the man at the top of the stairs was. Gray – *the man who died* – stood still for quite some time. But then JP seemed to buckle, as if he might fall to the ground, and Gray went forward and put his hands under JP's arms to hold him up. JP fell forward then, into Gray. I remember the sound of the two men sobbing. I stood to one side, shocked, shaken.

After a while, the two men separated and Gray looked intently at his friend. 'Aren't you going to say something JP?' he said. 'It's not every day an old friend rises from the grave.' JP was shaking. Would this be the moment? Would the shock of this revelation bring forth words from his mouth at last? He took a step back and sank into an armchair. Gray looked awkwardly at me. 'You must be Harry?' he said.

I frowned. 'You know me?'

'My mother told me,' said Gray.

'Your mother knows you're alive?' I said.

'Yes of course...' He glanced at JP. 'I couldn't have allowed her to think otherwise.' He moved towards JP and put a hand on his shoulder. 'I'm sorry JP.'

There was another long silence. Gray went over to the window. 'I knew you were coming,' he said. He pointed at a pair of field glasses on a table by the window. 'I've been watching, you see. My mother told me you'd been to see her a couple of times so I've been looking out and when I saw two men coming across the park, I … well, I recognised JP straight away and I wasn't sure if mother would keep the secret or if you'd work it out.' He looked intently at JP, who had buried his face in his hands. 'How did you work it out?'

'It was an old picture that JP had,' I said. JP looked up and dug into his pocket. He pulled out the picture and I took it and handed it to Gray.

Gray looked closely at it. 'Ah yes,' he said, 'That was taken here. This apartment belonged to my father. It seemed like a good place to … hide, or start a new life, whatever you want to call it.'

I took another look at Gray's face. When I'd walked into the room and saw the man at the top of the stairs, there was something about it that I recognised instantly, but I could see the changes too. Would I have recognised Gray if I'd passed him in the street? I'm not sure. His hair was a different colour – dark brown instead of childish blond – and it was cropped in tight to his scalp. Maybe it was the scowl I would have recognised – the way the eyes narrowed and turned down. It was there in the picture from years ago and it was there now. Your eyes don't change.

I could hear JP taking big gulps of air. He took his notebook from his pocket and wrote in it and held it up to Gray. *Why did you do this?*

Gray went to a sideboard next to the settee and opened one of the drawers. He rummaged around until he found what he was looking for. It was a photograph of a young woman sitting in the driving seat of a motor car. She was leaning forward towards the wheel, her shoulders drawn up, her long hair falling over her neck and behind her. She was smiling broadly, as if she were laughing at something the photographer had said. The woman was about 19. It was Sarah Brindle.

'This is the only picture I've kept from my ... previous life,' said Gray. 'I needed at least one reminder.' He looked at JP. 'We have suffered so much JP, haven't we? But at least you *went on.* You carried on living and signed up and went out to France, while I sought solace in ... you know, little white tubes.' He put the picture down on the sideboard. 'The pain increased. And it got worse. There was a time when I had no money and no food. It had all gone. I even refused help from my mother.'

I told Gray about our visit to Dan. 'Dan gave me money when I hadn't a penny,' he said. 'He's a good chap. But it wasn't enough. It wasn't enough to save me, I mean.'

He moved back to the settee and sat down again. 'They were going to kill me,' he said. 'Another week, another day maybe ... I couldn't sleep, my heart beat so fast that I thought some days it would jump out of my chest. It would have killed me in the end. I couldn't bring Sarah back to life, and I was too *frightened* to sign up and go to France in the hope that the Germans might kill me, so there was only *one other way.'*

Gray sat back in the chair. 'Mother and I discussed it. At first, she said it would be sinful, to turn my back on life and pretend I was dead. It was a sign of my ingratitude to God, she said, for everything he'd given me. But I had to tell her and she could see it for herself ... what the drug had done to me, and how much money I owed to people who would do anything to see that their debt was paid, and I told her about my ... pain and my need to be rid of it, and perhaps it was those words that made sense to mother. I remember her saying that maybe this was my chance for a ... rebirth. I could be born again and perhaps in the new life, there would be less pain.'

'But your mother identified your body,' I said to Gray. 'At the police station.'

Gray clasped his hands together. 'We didn't plan that at first. The idea was that I would simply disappear and no one would be able to find me, but it was mother who said 'your enemies must believe you are dead'. And she showed me a story in the newspaper about a young man who'd been hit by a tram on Victoria Road and the newspaper said that no one knew who he was.' He looked at JP. 'So she went to the police station and identified the poor young man in the mortuary as me. And she came home and asked to pray with me and told me to go and begin my new life.'

'*Those who sleep in death will be raised,*' I said.

Gray looked up in surprise.

I looked around the apartment. 'And you've lived here ever since?' I said.

Gray nodded. 'When people believe you're dead, when they *know* you're dead, it's surprisingly easy not to be seen.' A wistful smile came to his lips. 'You don't know this JP, but there have been a couple of occasions when I've been standing near you and *you never even noticed*. My hair isn't the same colour, I dress differently. I know what it's like to die and live in the afterlife.'

'We saw your grave,' I said.

Another rueful smile. 'Imagine what it's like for me,' said Gray. 'I've been down there too. It took me a while to pluck up the courage and then I could see the funny side. Who gets to see their own grave eh? I've got a peculiar sense of humour sometimes, all the practical jokes I used to play at school. Remember JP? Well, I could see the joke this time too. I bought some flowers and put them on my own grave. I couldn't resist. And the flowers weren't for me anyway, not really. There's a young man under that slab of stone and no one knows who he is. Perhaps, somewhere, his family are still looking for him.'

Gray leaned forward in the settee. 'I hope you can see why I had to do it JP,' he said. 'You and I saw what we saw and I'm a coward really and I realised that I could hide behind … death. It was either that or …' He tailed off. 'I have a kind of death and you have … your silence.'

JP looked up at his old friend and an emotion flashed across his face. I wasn't quite sure what it was. Anger? Not quite. Grief. Yes, possibly. Shock. *Shock*. Gray stood up and went to the window before turning back to JP. 'Mother told me about … how you were.' He turned to me. 'When was the last time he spoke?'

I looked nervously at JP. 'He hasn't spoken for … a long time,' I said. Gray went over to his old friend and crouched down beside him. He put his hand on top of JP's. 'Now that I'm … back, perhaps I can help you. To talk. And we will talk about the old days, before the war, before Sarah died, and we'll look at all those old pictures and maybe we'll laugh at some of the memories.' The emotion that had flashed over JP's face a few seconds before seemed to be gone now. His face was pale and blank.

Gray got up and went back to the window. I said something to break the silence. 'Did it work?' I said. Gray looked at me. 'I mean, has all of this worked?' I said. 'Faking your death? You are no longer addicted to cocaine?'

Gray said no, he wasn't. 'It wasn't easy though. But I took on a new name, I came to live here, I cut off contact with all my old friends and enemies, but it was a terrible struggle, the first few months. Mother helped and occasionally, when she thought it was safe to do so, she would come here. She's the only one from my *old life* who knows.'

He sat down in the chair. Moll went forward and sniffed at his hands.

'JP told me what happened,' I said. 'We … went to the theatre.'

Gray looked up from Moll. 'Then you've got some idea,' he said. 'You've got some idea why we've ended up here. Why I became addicted. It was because of what we saw in that corridor, at the theatre, I'm sure it was.' He looked at JP. 'We have to get this mended don't we JP? I mean now that I'm … alive. I suppose that's the right word.' He leaned towards JP. 'I'm sorry old friend. I will say it a thousand times until you believe me. I'm sorry because I was selfish. I went away and pretended to be dead. And it helped me, didn't it, but you were on your own.'

'What happened when the war broke out?' I asked.

Gray put a hand to his chest. 'I've got a dicky heart. I went down to the doctor's surgery with my papers. I had a new name, George Smedly, and the doctor listened to my chest and that was that. I'd have been no good anyway in the army because I'm a coward. That's why I'm here isn't it? I can cope with this – this fake death – but I couldn't cope with the real thing. I was too afraid to go to France so I hid behind a fake name and a heart that doesn't work properly.'

JP was looking at the window behind Gray and didn't switch his gaze. 'Will you tell the police?' asked Gray. 'Please don't, not yet. I don't want them to come after my poor mother …'

'I'm sure they'll understand,' I said, although I wasn't sure they would. I could see Chief Inspector Downs's face as he hissed the word *coward* at me. What would he make of a man who had faked his own death and hid in a comfortable apartment while his countrymen were killed in France?

Gray had turned to JP again. 'I want to help you JP,' he said. 'I want to help you in all of this, to find who killed Sarah. I thought hiding here would mend things, but it hasn't. Sometimes, I imagined what this moment would be like, when you discovered I wasn't dead, and then I was looking through the field glasses and I saw you and Mr Baker coming towards the building and I ... knew ... I knew that you were coming up here and I opened the door and left it open and stood here and waited for you and ...'

He put his hands up to his face. 'It's such a relief.' He smiled weakly. 'And who gets the chance to come back from the dead? I'm only the second person I know of who's done it.' He laughed but the laugh cracked. Then he fixed us with an earnest stare. 'But you mustn't tell anyone else. You're part of my secret now.'

I glanced at JP. Neither of us reacted.

'They would send me to prison,' said Gray. 'For lying to the police, for living this lie.'

'They won't send you to prison,' I said. *They won't do the same thing they did to me*, I thought. 'They may want to ask you more questions about Sarah's death,' I said.

Gray lowered his head. 'I go there quite a lot,' he said. 'In my mind's eye. To the theatre. I ask myself: why didn't I do this ... or that? Why didn't I move forward sooner? We were standing there watching the man in the mask ... stabbing Sarah and we were frozen. It couldn't have been more than a second or two, maybe even less, and I screamed 'they're stabbing Sarah!' and he dropped her body and slammed the door and it was locked.' He put his hand up to his face and rubbed his eye. 'I've remembered it a million times in this room.'

'You have no idea who it might have been?' I said. 'The person who killed Sarah?'

Gray shook his head. 'No. No. You've spoken to our

friends haven't you? Can you imagine any of them doing it? Elizabeth for example? She loved Sarah. Or Rachel? She's away with the fairies but she's gentle. And Dan, well, Dan's got a temper and he behaves like a fool sometimes, but it's all front. He's a good man. No ... it was someone else. Someone Sarah never told me about.'

'A stranger?' I asked.

Gray shook his head. 'No, I mean someone maybe who she ... knew perhaps and hadn't told us about.'

'You think it was definitely a man who killed her?' I asked.

Gray narrowed his eyes, like he was summoning up the memory. 'Well .... I thought I did. I mean, JP, you must see it in your mind's eye too. We're standing there and there's someone stabbing Sarah and I remember him, his arm raised and Sarah screaming and ... well, maybe I've *assumed* it was a man. All I know is that he slammed the door shut and I heard them struggling on the other side and Sarah is still screaming and I start to kick the door down, but it won't budge. And then when the police came a few minutes later and kicked the door in... there she was.'

Suddenly, JP moved. While Gray had been talking, he had been leaning forward, his eyes on the floor, but suddenly he sat bolt upright. Then he stood up and started walking towards the door.

Gray stood up and called after him. 'JP! Where are you going?'

JP did not look back. Moll followed him out into the hall. Gray did too. Then me. JP was standing out on the landing. Gray put a hand on his friend's shoulder but JP shrugged it off. 'What are you doing JP?' asked Gray. 'Stay here please. I still have a lot to tell you.' JP shot him a glance. Dark. Cold. Angry. Gray kept talking. 'I'm sorry. Please understand. I'm sorry. Sorry. JP. Please.'

JP started walking down the steps. I looked at Gray. 'I'll speak to him,' I said. And I followed him down the stairs and at the last minute, I glanced back. Gray was standing by the banister and I suddenly saw two images in my head. One was of the little, frowning schoolboy with the bob of blond hair, and the second was the same person, years later, the man he became. A man who died, then lived again. And there he was, the man at the top of the stairs, the man who shouldn't be there, a ghost transformed, by some unexpected miracle, back into a human being.

17

The truth about Gray left me in a state of shock and bewilderment. I remember, but only through a kind of haze, making my way down the stairs and reaching the foyer to discover that JP had hurried ahead and there was now no sign of him. And I also remember standing outside the building uncertain what to do next. I considered going back upstairs to the apartment and speaking to Gray just to check it was all true, that he had not died, that he had been, as his mother always wanted him to be, *born again* but I knew it was true. I had seen it with my own eyes. I knew that the story JP had told me, the story JP *believed*, was a work of fiction. The question was: what on earth would happen now?

I was particularly worried about JP's reaction and as soon as I reached my rooms, I sat down and wrote to him urging him to get in touch and tell me he was okay. Later, I sat and listened to the life of the building and the bustle of people and traffic outside and ran over the conversation with Gray. I did not, could not, understand his motivation, perhaps because I had never been an addict of drugs, or perhaps because I had never shared the religious mania of his mother. But I had enormous pity for the poor man. I could hear in his sobs, when he first saw JP, and I could see in his anxious face, that the decision to 'die' had not been taken lightly. He felt he had no choice. But I also knew that the police, particularly Chief Inspector Downs, was likely to take a different view, especially if they assumed, as I am sure they would, that he had hidden behind the name of another man to avoid being conscripted into the army.

In the days that followed, my anxiety was only heightened by the fact there was no reply from JP. Indeed, I heard nothing from my friend for two weeks, and the spring break had begun so I did not see him at university either. For a couple of days, I wondered whether I should seek him out at his rooms, or even go to see Gray again. But I think I was beginning to get to know JP better and knew there was little point in trying to harry him. I would simply have to wait.

As usual, my friendship with Corie was a consolation, but even she could not comfort me completely. A couple of days after the extraordinary meeting with Gray, she and I went to O'Henri's and she could see at once that I was distracted and told me that I was being a terrible bore. I smiled and tried my best, but I couldn't hide my distraction and despondency and suggested we make an early night of it. Corie pretended to sulk, but she took my arm and I escorted her back to her small flat and then walked back to my rooms. For a moment, I considered slipping into the park to see who might be there, but my mind was on other things. One thing only in fact: the boy who died and then lived, and his friend: the boy who never speaks.

My next contact with JP, when it came, was quite by accident. Over the spring break, he hadn't replied to any of my letters, and he wasn't in any of the lectures on our first day back. However, on the second day, I was leaving a lecture, when I saw JP coming down the corridor towards me. When he spotted me, he stopped and made as if to turn around and it reminded me of our very first meeting. But I am less tolerant now than I was then so I went up to him and put my hand on his arm. I asked him why he hadn't replied to me, and how he was feeling. For a moment, I thought he might run off, but I marched him to the pub on the high street. There, me talking and JP writing his jagged little notes, we discussed Gray and what we might do next. JP hadn't been back to see him but he had heard from Gray's mother and he showed me a polite, matter-of-fact letter from Mrs R asking to see us both at her home. I told JP it was important we saw her. I was interested to see what she might tell us about the role she had played in her son's deception.

But I was also concerned for JP and told him, not for the first time, that I knew a place where I felt *comfortable* and perhaps he would too. I wasn't sure what his reaction would be, but he nodded, and we left the pub and he followed me through the streets and there it was, up ahead: my favourite hidden place. And when I said the password to the doorman, I watched JP's face closely for any sign of discomfort or fear or disgust but he was inscrutable. He gave no reaction either when we got inside and realised – for there could be no mistake when he saw the room and the dancefloor and the arms entwined in arms – what kind of establishment I had taken him to.

As for me, I could feel my anxiety dropping away, as I always did. Outside The Cave, I was always concerned, in some way, that someone would realise the truth about me that I was forced to conceal – *the many truths*. But here was a place – perhaps the only place – where at least one of my secrets could be revealed. I ordered drinks at the bar and led JP to a table at the back, all the time keeping a close watch on his reactions. For a while, we simply sat and watched as men, of all ages, milled around and looked and looked away and looked again. Occasionally, I would ask JP if he was ok and he seemed to be. He sipped his cocktail and smoked cigarette after cigarette and his hair, swept to one side as always, shone in the light above our table. I began to think, cautiously: I haven't got it wrong taking him here.

I started to talk. I needed to talk. I told JP about all the concerns and doubts I'd had about him, and what we were doing, and I told him about my fears for him, and myself, and I told him every detail I remembered about my time in prison and how I'd got there. I told him about the commandment that guided me – *thou shalt not kill* – and I told him about the men who tried to convince me I was wrong: the red-faced colonels and parish councillors who sat on the tribunals and the chaplain who told me that killing Germans was a divine service. I told JP I could not accept that and I could not be a part of the war – any part of it. And then I told JP that I was worried he would hate me. He'd signed up in that first wave and he'd proudly had his picture taken on the way back from the recruiting office, and he'd gone to France. And I hadn't. JP reached into his pocket and took out his book and wrote a few words. *Who was right? Me for going, or you for refusing to go? You must feel no shame.*

It was a great relief to see JP write those words. I looked at him across the table. What an extraordinary man he was. I could see the slight tremble in his hand as he lifted the glass to his mouth, and I knew the scar was there under his jaw although it was too dark to see it, and I knew that war had taken the words from his mouth. I felt a surge of affection for him, and a desire to protect him too. I reached across, clasped at his hand, and told him I would get him another drink.

I was standing at the bar when someone tapped me on the shoulder. Roger. An acquaintance, someone I didn't particularly like. He had a habit of running a hand through his curly hair when he thought he'd said something amusing, which wasn't often. He spent the war writing reports of the action on the Western Front from a newspaper office in Westford Road; reports that I thought were rather vulgar and betrayed a kind of vicarious excitement at the death and the fighting. I didn't like him, if I'm honest, or what he did. But The Cave threw us together and we exchanged pleasantries. He glanced across at the table where JP was sitting.

'And who is your dark friend?' he asked. 'You've been sitting there for ages and he's not said a word.' He smiled and I got a glimpse of his brown teeth. There was a gap in the top row. 'Will you introduce me?'

I glanced at JP then back at Roger. Was this really the introduction to The Cave that I wanted for JP? I put my hand on Roger's sleeve as he started to make for the table. 'My friend,' I said, 'was … injured in France.' Roger smiled and headed for the table.

I think 'awkward' would be the best word for the encounter that followed. As was his wont, Roger sat heavily down in front of JP and started to *perform,* declaiming on many subjects of which he had only a cursory knowledge. At one point, he leaned over and put his hand on top of JP's and said loudly that the British government *owed* something to men like us. We had survived the bloodletting and lost friends just like everyone else and now we were home and had to resume our secret lives. The men who fought at the Western Front and loved other men deserved the same citizenship as the men who loved women – they'd stood in the same mud hadn't they? They'd shed the same blood, hadn't they? So why were they denied the same rights? I did not disagree with Roger but I could see that JP was discomfited. As usual though, Roger didn't notice or didn't care and became louder and more outrageous.

Eventually, perhaps when the novelty of JP's refusal to talk wore off, Roger became bored and also realised fairly quickly that he wasn't going to get what he wanted from

JP – and so he pretended to spot someone he knew at the other end of the room and slunk off. I wondered whether I'd done the right thing bringing JP here. His face betrayed no emotion. Occasionally, I would ask him if he was OK and he would nod and light a cigarette and scan the room and I thought I could detect a kind of curiosity in his face. But I thought, not for the first time: I don't know JP.

Then, just as I was beginning to relax, I realised I had probably misjudged the situation more than I thought. The room had filled up a little more and the conversation, and laughter, was louder and I had to push myself past groups of increasingly rowdy men to get to the bar where I ordered another two cocktails for JP and I. I then pushed my way back to our table but when I got there JP had gone. Suddenly, Roger appeared at my side, running his hand through his curls. 'Your silent friend left,' he said. A smile played on his lips. 'Perhaps he was bored of not saying anything.' I put my drinks down on the table. 'Did you see where he went?' I asked. Roger pointed at the door. 'That way,' he said. 'In a hurry.' Roger laughed again and said he would see me next time and went off to badger someone else.

I left the drinks on the table and got my overcoat and went out into the street. This was the second time JP had run off, first on the day he saw Gray resurrected, and now this. Perhaps I had forced the issue rather too quickly. Perhaps he was horrified by The Cave and would never speak to me again and, at that thought, I felt ... *panic*. I did not want to lose my new friend. I stood in the street for a few moments, wondering if JP might return, before I headed back to my rooms.

A couple of days later, there was a message from JP. *Forgive me for disappearing so suddenly. I would never have had the courage to go to a place like The Cave on my own and I'm not sure I will ever have the courage to go back. One of my duties in France was to read the mail of my men to ensure there was nothing unsuitable about their characters. It was a way to divert attention from my own secrets. I have arranged for us to meet with Mrs R on Friday at 5pm. JP.*

18

I was more than a little nervous about our appointment with the formidable Mrs R and what we might learn from her. On our first visit, I remember her proudly showing us the photographs of Gray, scowling under his thick hair. And I could not forget her telling us about the terrible day she had gone to the police station and saw the body of her beloved son. Was that a fantasy? A lie? What part had Mrs R played in the deception? As JP and I approached her house, with Moll the dog at our side, I thought again of the words Mrs R had read to us from Corinthians. *Those who sleep in death will also be raised.* I hadn't realised when she first quoted them to me that she meant them literally.

When we arrived at the house, Mrs R led us into the drawing room. It was just as I remembered it. The bible on the table by the side of her armchair. The pictures of Gray on the sideboard. The bowl of sweet peas and roses on the mantelpiece. They were dry and withered. Mrs R showed us to two chairs by the window then went to fetch some tea and for several minutes she fussed over us, piling sugar into the cups and pressing cake on us, and breaking some biscuits into little pieces for Moll. But I could see there were cracks in her civilised politeness. Her thin, pale hands kept going up to her neck and picking at the lace. I glanced at JP. He was sitting bolt upright, his hands clasped on his knees.

'I want to thank you for coming to see me gentlemen,' said Mrs R. 'I feel that … I feel … ashamed that I had to deceive you and everyone else.' Her hand went to the side of the chair. The fingers rested on her Bible. She looked at JP. 'Gray told me that the sight of him was a great shock to you JP. I hope that it has not exacerbated your … condition. I wish that we had been able to take you into our confidence.'

JP took out his book, wrote a few words in it, and showed it to Mrs R. *Why did you do it?*

Mrs R looked at the note then handed it back to JP. Tears were forming in her eyes. 'I did it because I believed I had no choice. I had been praying for my son. Praying and praying. He was not the boy I once knew, not the boy you knew. The drugs – *the Devil* – was in him and I begged him to reform, to give up going to the immoral places he frequented, but he spent all the money he could get his hands on, and I had no idea how to help him.' She glanced at the pictures around her. 'He was never the same boy after Miss Brindle was killed and I sometimes wonder if that was the moment when the Devil seized his chance, when my son was weak and grieving. He loved Miss Brindle dearly and he had to witness her terrible, violent death.' She looked up at JP. 'But you know that JP. You saw it too.'

'Were you able to find any help at all for your son?' I asked.

Mrs R shook her head. 'I tried. I tried. I visited Rev MacIver and I told him everything and he told me Gray was being punished for drifting away from God and his only hope was to be born again.' She leaned forward in her chair, pale hands lost in the folds of her dress. 'And that's when I had the idea Mr Baker. *Born again.* My son's only hope was to leave behind his old life, and his old acquaintances and temptations and start again somewhere else as *someone else.*' She put her hand up to her face. 'God forgive me.'

'And so you went to the police station and identified the body of someone else as your son?' I asked.

She nodded gravely. 'It was the final deception, the means to allow my son's rebirth. I spoke to him for weeks about it, begging him to start again. He owed a lot of money to people who would do anything to get it. I feared they might kill him and he feared it too. I think it was the fear that finally convinced him. As long as he was alive, those men were a threat to him, but if he was *dead* they would no longer be able to reach him. And so he agreed. We arranged that he would live secretly in my late husband's apartment on the other side of town and I kept a close watch for our opportunity. And then one day, there it was. A little snippet of news in the Daily Herald. The story of a young man who had been hit by a tram. The newspaper said that his identity was unknown but that he was around 20 years old with fair hair. There was an appeal for information and I thought: *this is it*. Gray moved to the apartment immediately and I went to the police station and they showed me the face of that poor young man and I told them it was Gray. I hope God can forgive me for doing it. I hope you can forgive me for doing it.'

She removed a handkerchief from her sleeve, dabbed at her face, and looked at me. 'It was a terrible ordeal Mr Baker,' she said. 'I felt guilt at what I'd done, and I feared that the real family of the man might come forward at any time and expose our deception. But no one ever did and so I went to the funeral of a man I never knew and pretended to be his mother and cried over his grave and in a way the tears were real, because I was crying over what we'd done. I had killed off my son, but I thought: it's the only way to give him life. And a poor boy lies in the ground up at the cemetery and no one knows his name.'

'We visited the grave,' I said.

Mrs R dabbed at her face again and put her handkerchief back in her sleeve. 'I go there quite often, and place flowers there, fresh anemones or roses, it's the least I can do. What must you think of me? But perhaps I can justify my offence with a greater good? You saw my son Mr Baker. He was reborn. I *had* to put him beyond the reach of the Devil.' She paused and thought about what she'd said. 'But perhaps I haven't.'

She looked at JP. 'I also hope, JP, that some good may come from this. Perhaps a renewal of your friendship with my son will help you to cure your illness, to break your silence. It is not only my son I have prayed for.' She looked intently at JP then lowered her eyes. 'It has been a terrible ordeal to see my son suffer. And I know that you have suffered too. Is it too much to hope that this episode may assist you both?'

JP wrote something. The scraping of his pen on the paper seemed loud in the small room. I could see what he had written before he passed it over to Mrs R. *We must decide what to do next.*

Mrs R looked at the words. 'We have committed a crime, my son and I,' she said. 'So many young men went to France to fight, like you JP and you Mr Baker.' I did not flinch. 'And I know many people will judge my son for hiding while the war was fought by other sons of mothers. But please, do not judge us. I prayed and prayed and this was the *only way*. All I can do is appeal to you that you will not do anything rash now you know the truth.' She sat back and sighed. 'It is a sin to lie, but I have always felt, in a way, that I was not lying, not really. I told you that I went to see spiritual mediums. I said to you that I hoped my son would communicate with me from the grave. And in a way that's exactly what he did.' She looked intently at JP. 'Will you see him JP? Will you see my son? He would like that. He would like to see you.'

JP nodded.

'Thankyou,' said Mrs R. 'He has been alone for so long, hiding away, with only his poor mother to talk to, and only now and again when I felt it was safe. Occasionally, we talked about him moving away to another country to live, when the war was over, but the selfish part of me couldn't bear that. To lose him like that. And I felt sure that the only way to keep him safe was to hide him away. We still do not know who killed Miss Brindle. Perhaps they are still dangerous.'

'Gray was concerned about his safety?' I asked.

'Desperately concerned Mr Baker,' she said. 'Not only were there many men to whom he owed a lot of money, every single day he worried about the mystery of who killed Miss Brindle. He told me several times that he felt he was being followed, and I wondered if the drugs might be affecting his intelligence and his memories – there were some days when he was not … himself. But he insisted there was someone watching him and he feared that one day they might strike in the way they did against poor Sarah. At least, this way, *our way*, he could hide and wait for the truth to emerge, if it ever does.'

I noticed how her eyes were two spots of colour in the pale, white face. They were burning bright, they were alight, and I wondered, as I sat there, about her extraordinary actions. Was I impressed by the intensity of her love, her unquestioning desire to do whatever was necessary to protect her son and keep him safe? Or was I a little afraid of it? Yes, I think the latter. *Afraid.*

We talked on for quite a long time. Mainly, Mrs R seemed to have a desire to go over and over what had happened and her motives, perhaps to justify them to herself but mostly to justify them to her God. She also appealed to JP several times to see Gray but not to go to the police or anyone else just yet. Speak to Gray first, she said, and then we can decide what we must do. Gray is still fragile, she said, he could still break, so we must tread carefully. JP nodded and I said we would arrange to see Gray and report back to her, and she seemed to be relieved at that. 'I thought I could save my son from death,' she said, 'by pretending that death had taken him. Please do not judge me.'

So: did I? Did I judge her? I wondered about that as we walked away from her house and I was inclined to feel some sympathy for her, as well as a little twinge of discomfort and fear at the intensity of her passion. I also had no idea how JP was feeling about it, other than the signs of anxiety on his pale, pinched face. But in the days that followed our visit to Mrs R we wrote to each other more frequently than usual. JP wrote that he was concerned about the consequences of Mrs R's actions, but he also wrote a little about his own love for Gray and his friendship with Sarah. Sarah, he wrote, was the first person he spoke to about *sensitive desires* and it didn't matter to her and being an intimate of Sarah also meant being an intimate of Gray *even though it was hopeless.* But we must press on, he wrote. Our motivation from the beginning was to discover the identity of the murderer, the unknown person he and Gray had witnessed killing their friend, and perhaps Gray's reappearance might help.

One by one, I added the letters to the others JP had sent me over the months and almost every night I would take them out, and I would read over them and as I did, I could feel the intensity of my concern, and admiration, for my silent friend. I longed to help him. I longed to help him recover his voice. The growing intimacy between us, unusual though it was, nurtured and grown through the letters, was also increasingly important to me. And, as I sat in my rooms, alone, with no one to judge me, I could also admit to my worry that, in some way I didn't yet understand, JP's reborn friend Gray could be a threat to our friendship.

19

JP wrote to me again a couple of days later and I detected a change of tone. Suddenly, he was determined to see Gray again and to discover what he could from his old friend about the day Sarah Brindle died. He told me he had already written to Gray and explained everything that had happened to us in the last few months: JP being pushed under the car, the threatening letter I had received, and our interviews with Elizabeth the nurse, Barbara the waitress and her sister Rachel and the tempestuous Dan. I remembered that phrase JP had used in his note to Barbara: *something wasn't there.* He was afraid his memory wasn't quite *right* and that perhaps he had forgotten a moment, or fact, that might be crucial to solving the mystery. And perhaps Gray could help uncover it.

JP arranged for us to meet Gray at his apartment and when we arrived, with Moll in tow, I could see at once that he was nervous. He said he knew of our meeting with his mother and asked if we had decided what we would do and what action we would take. I told him we didn't think it was the right time to go to the police, a decision which I suspected was driven by JP's distrust and dislike of Chief Inspector Downs. I shared those feelings but even so I wasn't certain we were doing the right thing.

At first, Gray wanted to talk about what it had been like to live in hiding. Sometimes, he said, he would put on his spectacles and his hat and pull his collar up around his face and he would go to the streets he knew as a child and look for people that were familiar. He could never speak to them, or make his presence known, but he had seen Elizabeth near the hospital and even bought a coffee at

Barbara's café and Babs had handed him his cup without batting an eyelid. Gray said that, in a way, it had become a game: how close could he get to the people from his previous life without them recognising him? It was also a way to ease the isolation. The secret life was a solution to his problems, but it was also a problem itself: how do you live as a dead man?

It was only after we'd been at Gray's apartment for some time that he brought up the subject of the day Sarah died. I suggested to Gray that he go over the day again in the hope that it might offer a clue and as Gray began to talk, sometimes stopping to control his emotions, I could see how much the murder of his friend had affected him. I also saw, not for the first time, the effect that JP had on those around him. There was something about the fact that he never uttered a word that made others pour words out and they poured from Gray that afternoon. Occasionally, he would go over to the window; sometimes he would stop and fuss over Moll but mostly he sat in front of us and talked, his eyes sometimes on me but mostly on JP. Slowly, his story of the day emerged.

'You remember, don't you JP?' he said. 'Sarah was appearing in a show and we'd gone down to visit her at the theatre. She was so excited, even though her parents did *not* approve. They considered it a disreputable way to earn a living and perhaps even as bad as the *most* disreputable. But Sarah was happy. That picture I showed you, of Sarah in the car, it was taken just a few weeks before she died and I'd never seen her so contented.'

He stopped. 'Do you want me to go over the whole day?' he said. JP nodded.

Gray continued. 'So we walked down to the theatre to meet her and toast her success and when we got there, the man at the stage door told us where she was. There was a flight of stairs up from the dressing rooms that led to a corridor and at the end of the corridor was a kind of store room where there were boxes of props and costumes, and I remember there was an old ventriloquist's dummy sitting on one of the shelves once. Funny how you remember the small details. He seemed to have his beady eye on us.'

JP put a hand up to stop Gray and wrote in his book. *Did you think there was anything unusual about Sarah that day?*

Gray looked at the note then shook his head slowly. 'I don't think so,' he said. 'As I say, she was happy wasn't she? Her dream of working in the theatre was coming true. I mean, she could be moody sometimes, and things had been tricky after I said we should just be friends. But it was water under the bridge. It was going well for her, whatever her parents thought.'

He stopped and put his hand to his face. 'You know what happened next don't you JP? We were coming up the stairs when we heard a scream. When we heard *Sarah scream.* I think I got to the top of the stairs first and I remember looking down towards the little store room.' He stopped again for a few moments. 'Sarah was on the floor, just inside the room, and a man was crouching over her with his back to us and he turned – I remember that, he turned around – and he had a mask on, and ...'

I leaned forward and asked a question. 'Was he wearing some sort of gown as well?' I asked.

Gray nodded. 'Yes. Yes, he was. It was the oddest thing. They found the gowns in all the boxes later, didn't they? No one explained that, why he should have put on one of the gowns, unless he was an actor or... I don't know. But yes, he was wearing the gown, and the mask, and he had his hand up in the air ready to bring the knife down again and I shouted... I shouted something and ran forward – we both did. But the man, whoever it was, he slammed the door on us and I could hear the lock being turned and I kicked it and kicked it and called out for Sarah but the door wouldn't budge.'

JP nodded and it seemed to be the first time he had moved in a long time. He had been following Gray's account intently, so intently. He gave a little movement of his hand to indicate to his friend to go on.

'You know what happened next,' said Gray. 'You ran downstairs to the street and the police were there within a few minutes. I remember them clattering up the stairs and the weight of them all brought the door down and there she was …' He stopped again and tried to control his emotions. 'There she was on the floor. I ran forward and kneeled down and … the blood. *The blood.*'

He stood up and went to the window and, with his back to us, it was only the movement of his shoulders that indicated to us that his emotions had finally got the better of him. I felt great compassion for him in that moment and sensed once more the terrible toll that the murder of Sarah Brindle had had on her friends. After a few moments, when the only sound in the room was Gray's sobs, JP got up from his chair and went over to the window and – it was a small movement but deeply moving – he rested a hand on his friend's shoulder and they stood there for a little while, the light from the window turning them into shadows.

When they sat down again, and Gray had composed himself, JP took out his notebook and wrote some questions which he passed to Gray. Did he remember the details of the mask? Not much, he said. Did he see the mask after the murder? No, it had been found in the street behind the theatre. Might he have any idea why the mask would have been thrown away? None at all. Did he know anyone who might hate or dislike Sarah? Absolutely not, he said, and at that point he again got out the photograph of Sarah, the one of her happy and smiling at the wheel of the car. And he looked at the photograph and said: how could anyone hate this dear sweet girl?

And with that, he put the photograph in the drawer and sat back down. Moll had been sleeping by JP's feet but when Gray slumped in his chair, she got up and went over and put her nose on his knee and, without looking at her, he stroked her head. But his eyes remained on the ceiling.

After he recovered, we talked a little more of his time in hiding. He told us there had been two reasons for the decision to fake his death. First, because of his addiction, but secondly because he became convinced someone was following him. He was interested to find out more about the threatening letter left for me – *We killed Sarah Brindle and we will kill you too* – and the day JP was pushed in front of the car. Someone, said Gray, was fearful we were getting closer to the truth and they were prepared to kill. Gray urged us to be careful. Before his 'death', there had been a couple of occasions when he suspected he was being followed. I asked him if he had caught a glimpse of the person who was following him, or had any clue to their identity, but he said no, the person fled. And who else could it have been, he said, other than the man who killed Sarah?

We left him alone after that and walked away and through the park. Perhaps it was because I had grown used to it, but the silence between JP and I was companiable now rather than troubling. At the gates, at the point where we went our separate ways, JP took my hand in both of his and for some time wouldn't let it go. And – once again, it had only happened a couple of times – I thought, with a start, that he was about to say something. He opened his mouth and narrowed his eyes and for a second or two I waited to see what would happen. But the moment passed. The strain seemed to leave JP's face and he let go of my hand. I watched him go up the path, Moll by his side, and wondered, again, if there would ever come a time when I would hear my friend speak.

20

The letters I received from JP after our visit with Gray gradually became a little longer and a little more reflective, as if he was slowly becoming more used to the idea of talking on paper. Sometimes, even though he had always appeared disinclined to discuss his experiences of the war, his short, sharp letters would turn to the trenches and, to my surprise, it was rarely the battles or encounters with the enemy that he wrote about. Rather, it was the moments of peace, solitariness, and *silence*, that seemed to linger in his memory. In one of his letters, he told me how struck he had been once by the sight of two of the men in his platoon laughing – *there was so little to laugh at,* he wrote, *and yet how wonderful that they still could.* In another, he described walking from his dugout and smoking a cigarette and, in front of him, as he stood there, a little bird, a yellowhammer, had landed at the top of the trench. *Oh, that little flash of yellow,* wrote JP, *that little flash of life.*

There were also a couple of letters about the treatment he'd received in the hospitals. *I would play a game with the doctors,* he wrote. *I would give them a sign that maybe I'd speak one day, but I knew I wouldn't. And some of the doctors were kind and well-meaning and they would use that phrase 'shell shock' but they didn't understand – how could they? I didn't understand. Sometimes, I'd think: how can anyone possibly know how I feel when I don't tell them? And other times I would think: this will end one day. But the first sound I make will be a scream.*

In return, although I was initially fearful of his response, I wrote to JP about my own experiences and I will always be grateful that there was never a hint of condemnation in his replies. I seemed to find consolation in the same things as JP. The birds that played in the prison yard. My few, precious books. And, I must admit, the beautiful faces of some of the other men. I also sang songs I remembered from my childhood and recited poetry and all of it helped. Mostly, I remember the cold, but I also remember the food. I have followed a vegetarian diet for many years – many of the men who refused to fight do – and so, even though the rations were already meagre, I had to reject some of the food I was given. I lost so much weight, but thank God, never all my hope.

And so, my relationship with JP continued to develop, although I couldn't help notice that, after the revelation that Gray was still alive, our friendship was not *quite* the same as before, for another element had been added to it. Gray and JP had been dear and close confidantes before his 'death', and, after our visit to Gray's apartment JP told me that he and Gray had begun to correspond. I could detect an intimacy between the two men that perhaps JP and I would never have. The lesser part of me felt something close to jealousy.

It did not even cross my mind at this point, I have to say, that JP's old friend might ever write to me but when I returned to my rooms one afternoon, one of the letters waiting for me was from Gray asking me if we might meet. He said there were subjects he wanted to discuss with me but that I shouldn't come to the apartment – he was concerned about too many people being seen there – and asked instead that we meet at the park gates and that we do so after 7pm when it would be dark.

We set up the meeting for later in the week and when I arrived, Gray was already waiting, a scarf pulled up over the lower part of his face. He thanked me for agreeing to see him and told me of his concerns for his mother, now we knew the truth. 'She is a good and caring woman,' he said, 'and she acted out of the best of motives. She was fearful of the harm that might come to me but also the shame. Please do not blame her for what she did.' Gray also made me promise once more that I would not go to the police, at least not yet, and I made the promise, a little reluctantly. I was still concerned that JP and I were taking on much more than we should.

Gray also told me about his concerns over JP. 'He's a very different man to the one I knew before,' he said. 'JP was always ... quiet but this vow of silence that he's taken – if that's what it is – it's different. I find it hard to understand.'

'I think his experiences at the front have affected him, profoundly,' I said. I told Gray the little I knew from JP's letters.

'I've no doubt it must've been terrible,' he said, 'and every time I think of it, I feel the shame that when he was out there, I was in the apartment, warm, safe ...'

He seemed uncertain about what to say next. 'I have nothing but respect for your position – you acted out of a belief in a principle, inspired by the Bible, and I have no respect for the men who put on their collars and robes and preach that it is God's work to kill Germans. You, *you* are the real man of God, motivated by the words of the good book. You are no coward.' He brought his hand up to his chest. 'I am the real coward.'

He walked into the park and we were silent for a few minutes.

'You know, it's funny that JP and I ended up friends,' said Gray. 'I was never one for books really and JP never had his nose out of one. I also ... I'm ashamed to say ... I probably bullied JP a little when we first met, and he wasn't the only one either. But I was immature, and I learned eventually.' He pushed his hands deep in his pockets. 'I remember once, JP and I ended up in a fight – nothing serious, and JP got the better of me. He's stronger than he looks and he held me down and said 'so that's that then' and it was. The bullying stopped.'

'JP told me about that,' I said.

Gray looked at me. 'Did he? Yes, I suppose he did. It was a turning point in our friendship. We became close after that, perhaps because we were different. Maybe I gave JP a little more confidence, to speak up, and perhaps JP gave me the confidence to stop acting big all the time.'

Gray suddenly looked at me very seriously. 'Did you know that JP has started seeing his doctors again.'

I hadn't known that and I felt a little surge of jealousy that I hadn't. I felt closer to JP than ever, but I would never be as close as Gray.

'I wonder perhaps,' said Gray, 'if he's gone back to the doctors because of the shock of seeing me, who knows, but I'm glad he has because we have to cure this … thing. This *problem* he has.' He looked at me earnestly. 'How long has he been like this? I mean, how long has he refused to talk?'

'I'm not entirely sure,' I said. 'I think it had begun even before Sarah was killed, and by the time he came back from the front, he had stopped talking completely. They tried everything in the hospital I think, forms of hypnosis, all sorts of things. None of it worked.'

Gray shook his head. 'Poor sod. Perhaps they'll be able to help him this time. It isn't … normal, but you hear about the damage that can be done to a man out in France. To a man's mind I mean.'

'I think there's more to it than it,' I said. 'In JP's case.'

Gray looked at me curiously. 'What do you mean?'

'Well, it's just something Barbara said to me,' I said.

'You remember Barbara? She's a waitress now at the café on the Highborough Road. She said JP *learned* not to speak about certain things and it stuck in my mind. JP was damaged by the war, and being a witness to Sarah's death, but it seems to me sometimes that he's had to be silent about many things for much longer than that.'

I wondered whether I should tell him about our visit to The Cave. We walked on a little and I found myself talking about it, carefully at first, then with more confidence as I could see that Gray wasn't shocked or angry. He'd suspected it, he said, before JP had, he thought. He told me about a time JP had visited Gray at his house, when they were still at school, long before murders and wars. They were 10 or 11 maybe and they were lying on the bed talking about cricket or something or other and Gray remembers realising in that moment that JP wasn't the kind of boy who was *traditional*. But they were still young and they weren't entirely sure what it was, and they wouldn't have said it out loud if they had.

We walked on a little further, and I looked at Gray and felt a little ashamed about being jealous. Gray was still thinking about the friend he once knew. 'Sarah once said it to me when we were together. She said she sometimes wondered why JP did not have a sweetheart and she thought she knew the reason. She knew many men with similar inclinations at the theatre and it was one of Sarah's most admirable qualities that she didn't care. In fact, she seemed to gather a certain type of person around her and put her arm around them. It was as if she could sense when someone was afraid.'

'You and Miss Brindle were dear friends weren't you?' I said.

'We were,' said Gray. 'She used to tell me about her ambitions to be an actress. Her parents did not approve of course. I'm not sure they really approved of me either. We went out a few times, to the theatre, but it was never anything serious and we were never quite *right* for each other. I think I realised it first. Sarah wanted to be *serious*. She was serious about being an actress and about having a boyfriend and I was … less serious. And so we had a conversation and I suggested we should be friends and she was fine about that. Her, JP and me. The gang of three.' He smiled at the memory.

We were near the top of the hill now, with the park behind us. 'There was another reason I wanted to see you,' said Gray. 'It's why I asked to meet you here at the park and not at the apartment.' He fixed with me with a grave look. No: grave is not the right word, now I think back. A better word would be fearful. He was afraid.

'I'm being followed again,' he said.

The wind suddenly seemed to pick up around us. 'What makes you think that?' I said

'Sometimes I think I could be imagining it,' said Gray. 'Sometimes I think it's because you and JP came to the apartment and I worry that someone might have seen you. But you know I like to stand at the window and look out with my field glasses?'

I remembered.

'Well, in recent days, I've seen the same man … hanging around the building. Sometimes he's further back in the trees. Sometimes he walks up and down the street.'

'Have you challenged him?'

'I haven't had the chance. Whenever I go downstairs, there's never any sign of him.'

'What makes you think he's watching you?'

'My suspicious, fearful nature I suppose. I wondered if *someone* saw you and JP come to the apartment and now they know I'm alive.'

'But how could they?' I asked.

Gray thought for a moment. 'I'm sure you're right,' he said, 'but I keep thinking about that letter you received, the one that threatened to kill you. And *someone* pushed JP under the car didn't they?'

'Yes,' I said. 'But how could they know you're alive?'

'Perhaps because they've been watching you ... and now they're watching me.'

'You should go to the police,' I said.

He shook his head. 'No. No. Going to the police means telling them I'm alive and that means telling them about my mother and then the men who are after me would come for me anyway. No. No.'

I tried to change his mind. I also tried to convince him everything would be OK, without actually knowing for certain that it would be. *Someone* had killed Sarah. *Someone* had tried to kill JP. *Someone* had threatened to kill me. And it was entirely possible that the same *someone* was now watching Gray. All three of us, I had to admit, could be in the most terrible danger.

I looked at my watch and suggested it was time to go back, but Gray seemed to hesitate. There was something else he wanted to do, he said. Would I come with him? We started to walk down the other side of the hill and out behind a church and back on to a path and suddenly I realised where we were. We were near the graveyard which JP and I had visited some weeks before. I knew then where Gray was taking me.

He stopped when we reached it and stood in front of the black marble. He took out a torch from his pocket and shone it on the stone. I read the words again. *Beloved son who parted this life September 16th, 1914, aged 21. Though worms destroy this body yet in my flesh shall I see God.*

'Why have we come here?' I said.

Gray did not look up. The light from the torch scanned the words again. 'Because I always do when I'm near,' he said. He put his hand out and touched the marble. 'I feel great compassion and pity for the man who's buried here. He has no name. There's a family somewhere who wonder what happened to him and only my mother and I ...' he looked up at me '... and now you and JP know the truth.'

He switched off the torch and we were plunged back into the dark again and a thought occurred to me: Gray did not want me to see his face. He did not want me to see the tears. He started to walk down the path again and after a few moments I followed. Ahead of me, Gray had his head bowed and his hands in his pockets. What a terrible curse it is, I thought, to be a man who has died.

21

After my encounter with Gray, I tried to lose myself in the routine of my life for a while. I attended my lectures, where JP and I sat next to each other and dutifully transcribed the details of British mercantilism and the Corn Laws. And occasionally Corie and I went to our favourite bar and sometimes I would look at her happy, confident face and think about how much I was keeping to myself. *Have I learned the habit of silence too?*

As for JP, I sensed that the focus of his attentions had changed a little. For months now, he had been determined to pursue our investigations into the murder of Sarah Brindle, and he was still determined to see it to its conclusion. But the revelation that Gray was alive had been a great shock to him and he was still, I think, attempting to understand it. In fact, I could see that JP and Gray had rekindled the intimacy they had enjoyed before Gray's troubles, although JP's inability to talk made it an eccentric type of intimacy (I knew that for myself). In one of his letters, which were becoming a little longer and more confident, JP told me that he and Gray met often – usually walking in a lonely part of the town and never at the apartment – and JP would listen to Gray talk and talk about his mother, and his schooldays, and the dreaded drugs, and his years of solitude and secrecy. And, inevitably, Gray would talk about the day Sarah died – over and over again. '*I listen with great attention,*' wrote JP, '*because I hope that, one day, I will see what really happened.*'

JP also told me in his letters that he was continuing to see his doctors at the military hospital and that they were still shining bright lights into his mouth and staring at the back of his throat in the search for a cause of his affliction – a cause which they never found. Apparently, one of his doctors had attempted a new technique called Regressive Analysis with the aim of uncovering childhood experiences JP might have forgotten. But JP told me he was not impressed with the process. Besides, he wrote, his childhood was a place to which he did not wish to return, even in memories. In every home, he wrote, there's silence about something. *'So is it any wonder I am silent?'* he wrote, *'when I was urged not to talk about anything that might be shameful? Don't tell your father. My parents taught me how to be silent.'*

I wished, when I received these messages from my friend, that there was more I could do to help, but there was little I felt I could do, other than send replies in which I expressed my concern. I was also beginning to feel a sense of frustration that we were not making better progress in our investigations and that we did not know more about the day JP was pushed in front of the motor car. And the day someone pushed a letter under my door. Against my better instincts, I wrote to Chief Inspector Downs and asked if there had been any progress in his investigations into the letter. But he wrote back to say that there were no clues.

But I did feel that perhaps there was *something* I could do when my lectures and drinks with Corie could not distract me. And so once or twice I went up to the old theatre without quite knowing what I was searching for and stood outside and walked around the building and stood where Rachel must have been when the mask was thrown out of the window. In a way, the wretched mask felt like the central mystery of the whole affair. Why had the person who killed Miss Brindle thrown the mask out of the window and stuffed the gown in the box with the other costumes? And why had he worn a mask and gown in the first place? It was an extraordinary thing to do, wasn't it? I felt sure, as JP did, that discovering the murderer's motives for his bizarre costume would uncover the murderer himself.

I also made a pilgrimage to Cadogan Square. It was in Cadogan Square that JP had been standing when he'd been pushed in front of the motor car and it suddenly occurred to me one afternoon that I should like to see it. I knew it was a busy place, with clerks and secretaries and shop workers rushing hither and thither, and I recall JP telling me it had been busy on the day he'd been there, waiting to cross the road. When I arrived, around lunchtime, it was just as crowded as ever and there was a newspaper seller on the corner trying to attract people's attention with the latest headlines. I went up to him, bought a Daily Herald, and engaged him in conversation.

'I believe there was an accident on this corner,' I said, pointing to the road in front of me.

The man looked up at me briefly as he sorted my change. 'There've been lots of accidents here sir,' he said. 'It's a dangerous bit of road, with the motor cars and trams coming tearing round that corner.' He handed me my change.

'I was remembering one accident in particular, in the summer,' I said. 'I believe it was an officer newly back from France. He was hit by a motor car.'

The newspaper seller thought for a moment. 'I saw it,' he said. 'Or at least I heard it. There was a commotion and a terrible noise and people were crowding round the gentleman. I'm not sure if he was badly hurt or not but they took him off the road and laid him over there.' He pointed to the pavement by the door to an office. 'They should have a constable here to slow the traffic down before someone's killed.'

I wondered whether I should say anything else, then decided I would. 'I heard that someone pushed the man in front of the traffic,' I said.

The newspaper seller looked up at me curiously. 'Pushed him? Why would anyone want to do that? It gets very busy here and he must've slipped or the crush was too great and … that's that.'

I tucked the Daily Herald under my arm as I prepared to leave but asked him one other question. 'You didn't see anyone … acting suspiciously?' I asked.

The newspaper seller stuck out his bottom lip. 'Don't know what you mean sir. There was a lot of fuss and a doctor was called from the surgery over the square there. The officer was out cold for quite a long time.' He looked at me searchingly. 'Are you a reporter?'

I shook my head and made to leave. 'Just a concerned citizen,' I said. 'Perhaps they will improve the road one day?' And with that I nodded to him and walked away.

Had I learned anything? Not really. In fact, I didn't even tell JP I had been to Cadogan Square, perhaps because my attempt at private investigation was so amateurish, although I did tell him about an encounter I had on the way back. I was coming down the hill away from the square when a large woman in a hat approached me near the entrance to a big grey building. She started thrusting a piece of paper at me. I took the paper before I could think what I was doing. 'Will you join our campaign sir?' she said. I asked to what she was referring and she pointed at the pamphlet. *Drugs: The Devil's Work*, it said. I glanced up at the building and read the sign over the door. Christian Association for the Control of Dangerous Drugs. I remembered. Mrs R.

That's when I heard her voice.

'Mr Baker!' It was Mrs R herself and she was coming down the stairs towards me. She was wearing a large green frock with, as usual, the black lace around her neck. She stepped into the street next to the large lady in the hat and put her hand on her arm. 'Have you come to join our association?' she said. She turned to the lady in the hat. 'May I introduce Mrs Hines, our secretary. This is an acquaintance of mine, Mr Baker. I have been telling him about the work of our group.'

Mrs Hines raised an eyebrow and smiled. 'Then we must tell you more about it Mr Baker.' She took my other arm so that I was flanked by the two formidable women. They began to lead me up the steps into the building. I protested that I had an appointment but they said it wouldn't take a moment and before I knew it, I was inside.

It was a municipal hall of some sort. Rows of seats led away to a stage at the far end. Draped behind it was a large colourful banner which read TRUST IN GOD. Before I knew it, Mrs Hines and Mrs R had led me up the aisle between the seats, explaining all the way about the work of their association. I feigned interest and reminded them of my appointment but it is no easy task to extricate yourself from gentlewomen on a mission. For 30 minutes or more, they told me about the evils of drugs and how cocaine had poisoned British soldiers at the front, and how cocaine and morphine led to *all kinds of moral depravity* and that concerned and responsible people must petition the government for action. I listened attentively, or appeared to, before spotting an opportunity for escape as more women arrived for the meeting.

Just as I was about to leave, however, Mrs R made another valiant effort. She took me to a table by the side of the door where there were piles of papers and pamphlets.

'Thankyou so much for listening Mr Baker,' she said. She picked up a pen and a piece of paper and started writing. 'We have meetings here every week and it would be *so good* if you were to come along.' She handed me the piece of paper on which she had written the details of the meeting that was due to happen the following week: *CACDD, Thursday. 7pm.* She then glanced back up the aisle at the group of women and moved in a little closer to me. 'I must say Mr Baker that I appreciate you *keeping our secret.* My fellow campaigners care deeply about the danger of drugs but they would be *horrified* to discover that the son of one of their number had actually been an addict.' She put her hand up to the lace around her neck and put her head to one side. 'You do understand I hope?' I said I did, put the piece of paper in my pocket, and made my escape.

I considered the encounter on the way home and realised again what a formidable woman Mrs R was. I had no intention of attending any of her campaign meetings, but I could understand the vehemence of her hatred of cocaine. She had seen for herself the power it could have over a man and I remembered Daniel describing his visit to Gray and the hollow version of a man he had found there. Perhaps, I thought as I walked down the hill, the only way to *really* cure Gray of his affliction was to discover who killed his friend. I didn't realise that I had just taken a significant step towards finding out the truth.

22

I was always a little surprised when Gray asked to see me rather than JP, and then I realised why he occasionally sought out my company. After all the years in which he had been isolated and hidden, he was finally able to see his old friend JP again and took great satisfaction from it, but there were frustrations too. JP could write notes and letters to Gray of course, but the two old friends couldn't really *talk* to each other, and perhaps I was able to offer Gray another way to express his frustrations and concerns. Gray was worried about his friend, mainly because he could compare the JP he knew at school with the JP he saw now, a man damaged by war and the murder of his friend. And the comparison, he said, was troubling. Gray would sometimes ask me if I thought JP would ever recover and I always gave him the same answer: I fear he may never speak again.

I think it was about two or three weeks after my encounter with Mrs R at the Christian Association for the Control of Dangerous Drugs that Gray asked me if I could meet him at the park again. He was amused when I told him about his mother's attempts to sign me up to her cause and for a while our conversation was rather light-hearted. It couldn't last, however. Gray told me he'd seen the stranger again, lurking around at his apartment, on one occasion pacing the street and looking up at the building and on another standing back in the trees. I tried to reassure him that perhaps the man was waiting for a girlfriend or some such, but Gray was unconvinced. 'It has to be the same man, doesn't it?' he said. 'The man who pushed JP under the car and the man who sent you the letter.' I suggested going to the police and he said it was impossible given how he'd hidden away for so long. Perhaps he could set a trap for the stranger, he said, but he would get him. He would find out who he was by hook or by crook.

I remember we talked for a little bit about who could possibly be responsible and I must admit that every person that JP and I had interviewed seemed most unlikely, with the exception perhaps of Daniel – I remember the fury on his face when he first accosted me at the theatre. Gray agreed – he could not imagine any of his old friends murdering Miss Brindle and terrorising him and JP. And so we discussed the possibility that perhaps Miss Brindle had met a man during her work at the theatre and it was he who had killed her. I glanced at Gray as he talked about Sarah and I could see various emotions appearing, then disappearing, from his face: frustration, anger, regret.

I suppose, in the end, we must have talked that afternoon for more than two hours because at one point I realised we had walked across the city for several miles and had reached the harbour area. At one point, Gray put his hand on my arm and said he wanted to thank me for the opportunity to be *normal.* But just a few minutes later he put his hand on my arm again, only tighter this time, and said he did not wish to go any further. He then guided me towards a side street that led back up to the centre of town and quickened his pace. I asked him what the matter was.

'I hadn't realised quite how close we'd got to the old part of town,' he said, glancing over his shoulder. 'There are places there where the risk of exposure would be considerably greater,' he said. He pulled at his hat so it sat lower over his face.

I looked back the way we had come. 'Are you afraid you're being followed again?'

Gray shook his head. 'No, not that.' He started walking

a little faster. 'There are places in the docks, places where I used to go to seek out …' He glanced at me and pulled his hat down even further '… the drug I needed.' He looked away from me. 'And *other pleasures.*'

'You went there to buy the cocaine?'

'Yes.' He took another glance at the street behind us. 'At first, my pharmacist was willing to sell me more than was legal, provided he was paid well for it, and then, after a time, he refused. And so, by that time, I felt I had no choice. *It was too late.* I had to find somewhere else, someone else who could give me … enough.'

'And you went to the docks?'

He nodded. 'There was an *establishment*, a block of flats near the harbour. A foul place really, but I became fond of one of the girls there and when I visited her, she said she could obtain what I needed. The money came from my mother at first – I gave her all kinds of excuses – and most of it was spent on visits to my friend at the harbour and the seemingly endless supplies she could obtain for me.' He suddenly stopped and put his hand on a wall, as if for support. 'I'm sorry if I appeared to panic Harry. I had a feeling, when I realised I was close to the docks again, that I might be *sucked back in* against my will. It's the power of it you see. The desire for it. I thought it would consume me once, and it would have had I not … died.' He took his hand from the wall and seemed to recover his stability.

We walked on then and Gray told me a little more about his experiences of the drug that seemed to control him for so long. At one point, he turned to me and spoke passionately about its effects and I thought for a moment that he was trying to convince me to sample it. 'It was the euphoria Harry,' he said. 'There is *simply nothing like it.* I would become alert to every detail around me and every detail in my brain and, while it lasted, I would sometimes think that I would never need to eat or sleep again.' He sunk his chin into his scarf. 'And then the effects would wear off. Sometimes after 30 minutes. Sometimes only 10. And I would be reduced to … myself again. Or worse. A more paranoid, anxious self, *and so* I would seek out more of the drug.' He looked at me. 'You see the endless circle, don't you?'

'What changed it?' I said.

'I started to run out of money, and my mother became suspicious, and I began to steal from her, and others, and when I couldn't obtain the drug, I would simply sit and *stare*. My poor mother tried everything to help but it was only after the men to whom I owed money began to seek me out and we feared that they might kill me that she suggested her plan. Her plan to pretend to be dead.'

'And you moved to your father's old apartment?'

He nodded. 'For the first few weeks, my mother locked the door whenever she left and took the key with her and she would bring me my meals and everything I needed. I thought of making an escape. I thought of smashing the window and climbing down the side of the building, especially when the need for the drug became strong and … almost unbearable. It was imprisonment I suppose, but after many, many months, I began to feel as if one day I might be normal again. There was a small trust fund that was left by my father and I hoped that one day I might be able to use that to re-emerge.'

'You hoped that one day you could come out of hiding, *as another person?*'

'I had hoped that, yes,' said Gray 'But … you've met my mother Harry. I began to realise that, unwittingly, I had walked into a trap of her making. A benign trap in many ways, a loving trap, but a trap nonetheless. My mother now had almost total control of my life and, because I had died in the official records and there was a gravestone that bore my name, I didn't even have a life to go back to.'

When I heard my new friend say that - *I didn't even have a life to go back to* – I felt great compassion for him, and sympathy too for the control that his formidable mother exerted over him. We talked about the ways in which he might establish a new life for himself, but by the time we reached his apartment he was in a despondent mood. Someone was out to kill us, he said, and they had killed Sarah Brindle, and we might never know the identity of the culprit. I tried to reassure him that JP and I had made considerable progress. But, in reality, I suspected Gray was right. And one thought persisted in my mind as I walked back to my rooms: *we may never know who killed Sarah.*

I wrote to JP at once and told him about my encounter with Gray, and he replied the following day. *Thank you for seeing Gray,* he wrote. *We must watch him and protect him.* JP also told me he'd been back to the hospital again. I was appalled to learn that one of the doctors told JP that his behaviour was self-indulgent and *disgraceful* in an officer of the British Army, but another, the psychiatrist called Hearns, had apparently proved much more sympathetic. Hearns was convinced the cause of JP's troubles was memory. *He asks me to put everything I can remember down on paper*, wrote JP, *my childhood, my first sexual experience, my time at the Front, Sarah's murder, almost everything, and he reads my scribblings and nods as if they are a source of great wisdom. But I do not hold out any great hope that he can help me. JP.*

23

In the days that followed, my studies and lectures were a useful distraction. The ancient history of Britain seemed like a comforting place to me, somewhere to which I could disappear, although JP and Sarah were never far from my mind. JP wrote to me to say that he wished to re-visit the McIntosh twins Barbara and Rachel, as well as Gray's friend Dan and the nurse Elizabeth Mackie, and ask them to go over their memories of Sarah once again. He told me he'd been thinking a little more about what his physician, Hearns, had told him about memory and felt sure that listening again to the accounts of his friends might help us to make progress, to distinguish the relevant from the irrelevant, to uncover the memories that were *true* and the memories that were *false.* It was there, wrote JP, that we would discover the truth about Sarah.

And so, one by one, we arranged to meet JP's old friends again and we sat and listened as they once more talked over their memories. For JP, the experience appeared to be intensely interesting, as if he were hearing the stories for the first time. But for me, I must confess, the meetings were awkward and disturbing. The problem wasn't the fact JP never talked – I was used to that now – the problem was that I felt as if I was now an accomplice to a particularly unpleasant type of deceit. I had to sit and listen to Barbara, Rachel, and the others talk about their grief for Gray while all the time I knew the truth. The meeting with Dan was particularly uneasy. I could see how upsetting it was for him to recall his memories of Gray. Didn't we have a moral obligation to tell him the truth, that his old friend was alive? Or was the obligation to Gray stronger? Could we tell the world Gray was alive when he was still too afraid to come out of hiding?

I wrestled with the same moral questions when we saw the twins, Barbara and Rachel, but I was prepared to be led by JP who told me in one of his letters that we mustn't break Gray's trust. When we met Rachel, JP seemed determined again to hear her account of the incident with the mask. Barbara on the other hand spent most of her time reminiscing about her schooldays with Gray and Miss Brindle and the others. Leaning over the table at the High Street Grill, she told us again about the time Gray had left the dead mouse in her desk and some of his other antics and practical jokes and said Gray's friends had indulged him even though he didn't really know when to stop.

Elizabeth Mackie was in a similarly reflective mood when we met her at her rooms near the hospital. JP had taken his mongrel, Moll, with us and Miss Mackie would occasionally lean down to stroke the dog's ears as she talked again about Sarah. She felt sure, she said, that Sarah had been seeing a boyfriend before her death and was worried at the time that her friend had been struggling to shake him off. But Sarah was such a loving soul, said Miss Mackie, that she would never speak ill of anyone, even a persistent boyfriend who wouldn't take 'no' for an answer. Miss Mackie also said she sometimes wondered what would have happened to her friend had she not been murdered, what kind of life she would have led. She thought Sarah would almost certainly have had a great future as an actress. But Miss Mackie also said that she wondered, sometimes, if she and Sarah would have worked together after the war broke out. Perhaps they would have volunteered in the hospitals side by side. Miss Mackie could imagine her friend out there in France, in the dressing stations, in the dirty white tents, offering comfort to the men.

Miss Mackie was the last of JP's friends we met and JP seemed satisfied with the process. In one of his letters, he told me he wasn't entirely sure why he'd asked his friends to go over and over what had happened, or why he'd asked Gray several times to do the same thing, but he felt certain that the road we were taking was the right one. In his letter, he also told me a little more about his meetings with the psychiatrist, Dr Hearns. Hearns was convinced JP needed to undergo a process of *un*remembering. *I am not convinced,* wrote JP, *but what he says about the workings of memory is fascinating. He says that not only can memories be consciously forgotten but that, by a different process, memories can be placed in the brain that are not true, sometimes through stress or trauma. He says it is one of the keys to understanding my condition. I must learn to adjust my memories, I'm told, for the sake of my sanity.*

In the days that followed, both JP and I had a considerable backlog of work to complete at university and spent a few contented hours in the library researching the minutiae of the career of Pitt the Younger. There were times in the early days of my friendship with JP when I found his silence awkward and oppressive, but I had known him for long enough now to find it companionable, especially when we were both lost in books. Occasionally, JP would pass me a message with a recommendation or a comment, but mostly we sat in complete quiet, broken occasionally by the sound of our pens on paper or other students coming and going. I would have been happy to stay there for weeks.

It was only when I got back to my rooms at the end of the day that my mind returned to my worries. I would lie in bed and mull over the progress, if any, we had made in our investigation into Sarah's murder. I was worried too about the circumstances around Gray and the fact that we were now, in my view, complicit in his deception. Since my encounter with Gray's mother at the Christian Association for the Control of Dangerous Drugs, Mrs R seemed to have made a friend of me or rather she had begun to see me as a potential recruit to her cause and had been regularly sending me more pamphlets warning of all kinds of drugs and appealing for money to fund their campaigns. And so, without telling JP what I was doing, I wrote to Mrs R and, as politely as I could, asked her whether she might one day convince her son to come out of hiding and face the world again. Her reply, when it came, was forceful. 'We must not exert pressure on Gray or open him up to temptation,' she wrote and, in short, swirling sentences, exhorted me, in the name of God, to remain silent.

For a while, I decided I would simply have to obey Mrs R's appeal and that it wasn't my place to force Gray from hiding. But then I would remember the faces of Rachel and Dan and the others when they spoke about the friend whom they believed to be dead, and I decided I would make one more appeal to Gray himself. He had warned JP and I not to come to the apartment in case we attracted attention, and I knew he was anxious because of the stranger who had been watching the flat, and so I wrote to him and requested a meeting at the park the following Friday.

When we met, Gray told me straight away that he knew what I was about to say.

'You've come to tell me to give myself up, haven't you?' he said.

'Give yourself up?'

'Well, admit the truth,' he said. 'Come out of hiding?' He smiled. '*Rise from the dead*?'

'I think it would be for the best,' I said. I told him about our meetings with Rachel and the others.

He listened carefully but shook his head. 'It wouldn't work Harry. Think about it. It is announced that I am alive, and first, my mother is arrested for perjury or perverting the course of justice or some such offence and then all those men who thought I'd died, all those men who thought they would never get their money, they would start loading their guns and sharpening their knifes. Their revenge has only been postponed Harry.'

'*Then let us help you,*' I told him. 'JP and I. We can get the money together.'

Harry shook his head again. 'Never,' he said. 'It is a *great deal* more than you, or my mother, could afford. I worked my way through a lot of drugs Harry, given to me by the girls who I started to think of as friends. But they weren't my friends. Their aim was to give me drugs with the promise that I could pay later and then suddenly I was told the debt was due and I realised quite how much it was. An impossible amount even if I worked every day for the rest of my life. That's when my mother and I came up with our plan, after I'd confessed everything – *everything* – to her. If I was to come back now, the debt could only be repaid with violence I'm afraid. For a long time, after my supposed death was announced, I was worried they might come after my mother, but she's not a rich woman. Perhaps that was the only thing that protected her.' He shook his head again. 'This is the only way.'

'Then we shall go the police,' I said. 'Name these men. Have them arrested.'

Gray was laughing now. 'Forgive me Harry, but you are being terribly naïve. If we go to the police, that would only hasten the revenge, and this time, my death would be *real*.'

I sighed in frustration. 'You cannot live like this forever

Gray.'

'That's true,' he said, 'but simply stepping out of my fictional grave and announcing my return is not the answer. I also accept that I cannot skulk around the apartment forever either, looking over my shoulder all the time. And that stranger, whoever he is, who's hanging around the street outside the apartment makes me suspect that my time is running out.' He looked at me earnestly. 'My mother and I have talked about it. Now that I'm cured of my addiction, at least I hope I am, the plan is to leave the country and start a new life abroad.' He put his hand on his shoulder. '*Please* give us time to formulate that plan. My mother told me about the letter you wrote to her. She is anxious you will go to the police.' He squeezed my shoulder. 'Please don't. We haven't known each other for long Harry but promise me that you remain silent for now and give us more time.'

I looked at his anxious face, shaded as ever by the hat pulled down low over his forehead, and told him he had my word. We continued to walk around the park and the conversation turned to the meetings that JP and I had had with his friends. Gray was most interested but doubted whether Miss Brindle's murderer would ever be found. He also talked a little about Miss Brindle herself. She had a wonderful influence over people, he said, an ability to convince them to join in her schemes and larks and he felt sure she would have made a very great actress. I asked him what he felt when he remembered his friend and he thought for a moment. The usual mix of emotions one feels with friends who are gone, he said. Regret, he said, that they didn't have more time together. And affection. But guilt mostly. Guilt that he'd left her side and hadn't got up the stairs in time to prevent her murder, and had to see something that a friend should never see: Sarah being stabbed to death in front of him. Yes, he said, what I feel mostly is guilt.

24

My meeting with Gray in the park stayed uppermost in my thoughts for several days, mainly because I still wasn't sure that we had resolved it in the right way – could Gray really hide from his enemies for the rest of his life? I wrote to JP on the subject in the hope that he might see my point of view, but instead my friend told me to leave well alone. What's more, he appeared to be rather irritated that I'd seen Gray without consulting him. I remembered the feeling I'd had that JP might not be telling me everything he knew. But it also crossed my mind that part of the reason JP might be silent was his need to *control* events. One can't control conversations. Notes on paper, on the other hand, are much more straightforward. But if JP had a controlling side to his character, then I had a rebellious one. I was developing ideas and theories of my own.

I must admit, though, that I was not completely unsympathetic to JP's concern for Gray. We could not know the potential consequences of Gray coming clean. Did his enemies suspect he was alive? I wondered whether we should be keeping a watch on his apartment ourselves, but in the end I realised that might put Gray in even more danger. I also felt that all the unanswered questions we faced, including the question that had started it all – *who killed Sarah Brindle?* – were intertwined in some way that we hadn't recognised yet. Was the man, or woman, in the street outside Gray's apartment the same man, or woman, who killed Sarah Brindle?

In the meantime, I sought comfort in familiar pleasures. There were a few trips to the park and I also saw Jamie, the man I'd met in the bar when I'd been out with Corie.

We talked about the police raids that sometimes happened at The Cave and he banged his fist on his knee and said it was outrageous that men could go out to France and fight and then be arrested in a place like The Cave. 'One day there will be freedom for men like us!' he said, and, in my small sitting room, for that moment at least, I believed him.

The occasional nights with Jamie helped to keep my brain on an even keel, but I'd also started to go for long walks across the city. It was a chance for me to order my thoughts and I slipped into the habit of walking by some of the places that had featured in our investigations, as if the stones of the buildings might somehow give up the truth. I would walk up through the town and across Cadogan Square where JP was pushed in front of the motor car. Then I would head down and through the graveyard and linger for a while by the memorial to Gray – no, not Gray: the memorial to a stranger. And then, finally, I would walk past the theatre and imagine JP and Gray standing at the door on the third floor and watching, in horror, their friend being murdered. The long, solitary walks didn't achieve anything in particular except I was beginning to feel that I had seen, or heard, *something* that was significant but that I hadn't yet recognised it as such. It was if I could hear the peeling of a bell from over a hill and the more I tried to head towards it, the softer it became.

I came back from one of my long walks one afternoon to find a message from JP. It was another short description of some of the treatments he'd been undergoing at the hospital under the guidance of Dr Hearns. *Some of the doctors are the most useless hacks,* he wrote, *and I struggle to summon up respect for them. One of them told me that, although he was sure I'd had 'a very trying time' at the Front, I must make a 'conscious effort to put it behind me', and it was all I could do to stop myself from punching him in the face. Did I fight for him? For his right to tell me to pull my socks up?*

Elsewhere at the hospital, JP's treatment seemed to have been more fulfilling. He felt doubly sure, he wrote, that his memories – remembered and suppressed – were not only the key to his troubles, but also the key to the mystery of Sarah Brindle. And yet he didn't know *how*. He kept going over his memories obsessively with Dr Hearns, he told me, looking for any inconsistencies or recollections that didn't make sense, and the memory that kept recurring to him was the memory of that childhood rhyme that had haunted him for years now. Those macabre few lines about the man without a face. *Sometimes*, wrote JP, *the men would hum that damned nursery rhyme in the trenches. God knows why. It was something familiar and anything familiar was a kind of balm to us.* JP ended his note by saying he would be in touch if his therapy at the hospital uncovered anything that was helpful.

I doubted it would and suspected JP's obsession with memory was a blind alley. We had seen his friends many times and they'd told us over and over again what they remembered. JP and Gray also had the *same* memories about the day Sarah Brindle died: for a second, perhaps two, they had seen a man kneeling over Miss Brindle and stabbing her before the door was slammed in their faces. They both remembered the gown. They both remembered the mask. I couldn't see how we were ever going to solve the conundrum. *And yet.* I could hear the sound of that bell over the hill. And so I left my rooms again and went for another of my long, thoughtful walks.

If I had expected that the inspiration, when it came, would strike me on one of those long walks, I was wrong, because it arrived while I was sitting at my little desk by the window. My papers and books had got into a terrible state over the last few weeks and I'd dedicated the evening to sorting them out. It was a pleasant distraction and occasionally, when I found a book that particularly interested me, I would stop and smoke a cigarette and read a page or two before putting the book on the shelves. I also went through my papers and sorted them into categories before putting them neatly away in the drawers. The order that slowly emerged from the chaos was soothing.

And that's when it struck me. It was right there on the desk. Surely it was. I rummaged round in the right-hand drawer looking for the other piece of paper I'd put there just a moment before. Here it is. Yes. The more I looked at the papers, the more I was certain. No, not *certain*. But there was enough there to make sense, to raise suspicion. I must have seen these papers a dozen times or more without noticing anything and now, with a surprising clarity, I could see the connections, as if my subconscious had suddenly told my conscious brain what was going on. There. And there.

I sprang to my feet and went to fetch my coat. *I would resolve this matter right now*, I thought. Then I paused. Could I be sure? Should I go to the police? Or at least tell JP? I thought of his irritation when I'd gone to see Gray without consulting him. I could also imagine Chief Inspector Downs's contemptuous face – he wouldn't believe a word of it.

I went back to my desk and looked at the papers again. Yes. *It was there.* I hadn't imagined it. I could go right now and establish the truth of this myself and *then* go to JP when I knew beyond doubt that I was right. I picked up the pieces of paper, folded them carefully and put them in my pocket. This would be the most unexpected revelation if I was right, but I was resolved. I was more than an assistant. I had made my decision. I made sure the papers were in my pocket and, before I could change my mind, left my rooms immediately.

25

Mrs R seemed pleased to see me. Perhaps she thought I'd finally read all the pamphlets she'd been sending me and was ready to be converted to her campaign on the dangers of drugs. She ushered me into her sitting room and began with her usual chit-chat, but I was determined to get straight to the point. I put my hand up as a sign that she should stop talking and she looked at me, a little surprised.

'I have something I must discuss with you,' I said.

She put her head to one side. 'Indeed?' I could see that she was slightly taken aback by my abruptness. 'I hoped, Mr Baker, that we were going to talk about my work at the association and how you might help? There is a lot that needs done and …'

I interrupted. 'This is not about the association,' I said.

She straightened her dress and looked at me, confused. 'I see,' she said, attempting to resume the civilities. 'Well, it's good to see you whatever the reason.' She glanced at me sideways. Something had changed in her attitude, something subtle. A little hardening in her eyes. How thin is the veneer of politeness, I thought.

'I've come to talk to you about Gray and Sarah,' I said.

She nodded at that, but her face had hardened a little more. She put her hand out and indicated that I should sit down. She sat down opposite me and patted her dress. 'I hope Mr Baker,' she said, 'that you haven't come here to try to convince me again to go to the police and tell them the truth about my son. I read your letter and I understand your concerns. But I know my son better than you do, and I made my thoughts perfectly clear in my reply.'

I patted my pocket and pulled out a piece of paper. 'You

certainly did,' I said. 'I have your letter here.' I held it up. My hand was shaking a little.

She sat back in her chair. 'Then you will understand my feelings. We had no choice. *I had no choice.* My son was in the grip of the Devil, Mr Baker, and, although I prayed for an answer, there was only one way. I did not *want* to go to that cold room at the police station and look at the body of that poor boy. I did not *want* to stand by the graveside and weep for a man I never knew. And Gray did not *want* to hide away and live the life of a dead man. But we had no choice, and I appeal to you – as I have appealed to you before – to respect the decision we were forced to make.'

I put the letter in my lap, unfolded it and flattened it down. 'I respect the decision you made madam,' I said, 'but my concern is what you might have been prepared to do to protect the integrity of your decision.' I looked up at her. 'To protect your son.'

She straightened in her chair. 'Anything Mr Baker. I would do anything to protect my boy, and I did. As I said to you before, I felt ashamed that I was deceiving his friends. Mr Allgood, and everyone else. My instinct as a Christian told me I must never lie. My instinct as a mother told me I must.' She put her hand to the table by the side of her chair and rested it on the Bible. I glanced from the book to the pictures of Gray on the sideboard and felt my first twinge of doubt. Was I sure about this? *Was I wrong?*

I looked down at the letter again. 'You said in your letter, madam, that we must not exert pressure on Gray or open him up to temptation, but it was not what you said in your letter that strikes me, but how you said it.'

Mrs R's hand drifted from the Bible up to her neck and began picking at the lace. 'I'm not sure I follow your meaning Mr Baker,' she said.

I glanced at the letter again, the short, sharp sentences, the swirling style, the jabs of the pen at the full-stops and commas. 'This letter was written in haste wasn't it? And in some anger? You were afraid that I was going to tell the truth about Gray being in hiding, and you dashed this letter off so that I would receive it as soon as possible. You may not have thought twice about sending it.'

'I certainly did not think twice,' said Mrs R. 'I was afraid that you, or Mr Allgood, would go to the police and expose my son to terrible danger. Why on earth would you imagine I'd think twice about sending the letter?'

I held the letter up for her again. 'Because there was a chance that I would notice,' I said.

She narrowed her eyes. 'Notice *what*, young man?' she said.

'The similarities. It was the same the day I met you at the Association for the Control of Dangerous Drugs,' I said. I put the letter back on my lap.

Mrs R said nothing. Her hand was up at her neck again, the pale, white fingers standing out against the dark, black lace, as they always did. She glanced at the letter then back at me. She appeared to be composed. It was just the hand, that hand at her neck, that seemed to signal something less certain.

I went on with my explanation. 'I came inside the association's building, do you remember? You were most solicitous and told me all about your campaign and wrote down the date and time of the next meeting.' I went into my pocket again. 'This is what you wrote for me.' I read it aloud. *CACDD, Thursday. 7pm.*

Mrs R briefly glanced at what she'd written, then looked back at me. 'I believe that is the note, yes. What importance does it have?'

I put the paper down. 'It had no importance at all, not on

its own. That day at the association. I listened as patiently as I could to your lecture about drugs – indeed, I was sympathetic to some extent because I knew what your son had experienced. And when I left the association, when I was allowed to leave, I went home and put the note in a drawer and thought no more about it.'

She leaned forward in her chair. 'You *should* Mr Baker. You should think about it. The campaign – *the war* – against drugs is only beginning. You know what my son has been through, you know the temptation he still faces. *That* is what drives me, love for my son and concern for the sons of other mothers who may one day face the same thing.' There it was. In her face. In her eyes. The passion. The fire. The emotion that had made me a little afraid.

'I've no doubt about the concern for your son, madam,' I said.

'Then what is this about Mr Baker?'

'It's about the letter A,' I said. 'That's what made me notice. It's here on the paper. *CACDD, Thursday. 7pm.* And it was there in the letter that was pushed under my door. It took me a while to realise and then I remembered the style of it. *WE KILLED SARAH BRINDLE AND WE WILL KILL YOU TOO.'* I looked up at Mrs R and waited for her reaction.

She said nothing. One hand was resting on her Bible, the other had drifted up to her neck. But there was no sudden look of guilt. No sudden confession. Her face was still and expressionless and I felt another, deeper twinge of doubt.

'I think perhaps, Mr Baker, you're going to have to explain what you mean,' she said.

Another stab of a doubt: *was I right? what if I was wrong?* I put my hand up to my brow. Sweat. Cold sweat. I must go on, I thought. Say it out loud to see what it sounded like, if it sounded true. 'I suspect you tried to disguise the writing when you wrote the letter, but it wasn't *quite* enough. There was something about the little stroke of the A, the curl at the end. And that wasn't the only thing, it wasn't the only connection, it wasn't the only thing that hit me.' I gripped the paper in my lap. Do not let her see your hand shaking. 'There was a quality, something about the manner of the letters too. One word: *'We'. WE KILLED SARAH BRINDLE AND WE WILL KILL YOU TOO.* It was in the letter you sent about Gray too. *We must not exert pressure on Gray or open him up to temptation.* It *sounded* like you. That's what struck me, all at once. The letters *sounded* like you.'

Mrs R unclasped her hands, but she was still calm. There was none of the anger and heat that flamed up when she talked about drugs or saving her son from temptation. Instead, she was as still as I'd ever seen her. I, on the other hand, had started to fidget. All I could feel was doubt, uncertainty. If I'd spoken to JP before coming here, perhaps he would have pointed out the flaws in my theory. It was flimsy. *Ridiculous.* There was nothing to it. I was an idiot.

Mrs R spoke. Finally. 'Would you let me see those letters?' she said. She put out her hand.

I folded the letters up and put them back in my pocket. 'I'd rather not,' I said. 'I intend to take them to the police and put my accusations to them. But I wanted to come here first and ask you whether you wrote that threatening letter.'

Mrs R withdraw her arm. 'Then ask me,' she said.

I shifted in my chair. 'Did you write it?'

'*I did not write it,*' she said. 'And presumably the police are continuing their investigations to determine who did.' Her voice had lowered. 'At some point Mr Baker,' she said, 'you will have to go to the police and put your accusations to them and I suspect they will be dismissed *very quickly*.'

'I suspect you may be right,' I said. 'The Chief Inspector doesn't hold me in very high esteem. But I will leave here and go to the police station anyway.'

'And when you get there Mr Baker,' said Mrs R. 'you will also have to explain to the police *why* I would send that letter.' Her upper lip had risen slightly, just enough to expose her teeth, and I thought of the polite veneer again, the surface, the covering. She would pretend her son was dead. She would lie to the police about the body of the young man killed by the tram. She would weep at his graveside. And she would write a threatening letter and push it under my door when she thought her secret might be exposed. I looked at her hands. Thin. Pale. What other *necessary steps* would she take? She would notice JP walking past the offices of the Christian Association for Control of Dangerous Drugs and she would follow him up the street to Cadogan Square and she would mingle in the crowd by the junction and put out one of her thin, pale hands and she would give JP a firm, hard push and, when he fell in front of the car and the brakes screeched, she would step back and become one of the crowd again. I could feel a kind of panic rising in me. A horrible, fearful panic. This woman, Mrs R, she would do something else to protect, or avenge, or save her son. She would be jealous or fearful of a woman for whom her son had affection, a woman who might one day take Gray away from her. She would follow the young actress up the stairs and put a mask over her thin, pale face and kill her.

I tried to talk, but just one word came out, over and over. 'I... I... I...' Mrs R has risen from her seat and she put a hand out and clasped my shoulder. I could feel her fingers pressing into my flesh. 'I will go to the police and ...' I put a hand out to the sideboard to steady myself. 'The police will rule on the …. truth … or otherwise. I will …' Speaking was almost impossible. I couldn't even breathe. I got three more words out. 'I will go.'

I stumbled to the door. Mrs R was telling me I was ill, telling me to stay, telling me the police wouldn't believe me. She may have said other things too. I'm not sure. I had to get to JP. I should have spoken to him first. But I would find him now. I got out of the house, and down the path, and out of the gate, and broke into a run. A woman pushing a pram glanced at me sideways, slightly alarmed. My chest was heaving. No doubt my face showed my emotion: a kind of terrible certainty. Mrs R had killed Sarah Brindle. Mrs R had killed Sarah Brindle.

Where could JP be? I hurried to the campus and checked the library, bursting into the room, still breathing heavily. The librarian looked up from her desk in alarm. JP wasn't here. I tried the tutorial rooms. Nothing. I had never been to his private rooms, I wasn't even certain where they were, but it was Rogerson Court, I thought, so I ran there. I stopped the doorman. Was Mr Allgood in, I asked him. He looked me up and down as my chest heaved. Mr Allgood was out, he said. I had nowhere else to look. I would have to leave a message for JP and tell him my suspicions. I asked the doorman for paper and envelope and wrote a brief note. 'Will you give this to Mr Allgood as soon as he returns?' I said. The doorman gave me another disapproving look and said he would.

I started walking down the street, still anxious, still breathing heavily. Should I go to the police now? Right now? No. I had to speak to JP first. I didn't want to repeat the mistakes I'd already made, thinking I could act on my own. I reached my rooms and opened the door. I was exhausted. There was an envelope on the doormat. I knew.

I snatched it up. It was from JP. *Meet me at the theatre at 7pm.* I looked at my watch. It was already past 7. Would he still be there? I would try. I pushed the note in my pocket and headed straight out again.

It took me around 15 minutes to reach the theatre, running some of it, walking when I could no longer run. At times I thought my anxiety would kill me. I could still feel the cold certainty I'd felt when I imagined Mrs R pushing JP in front of the car and … stabbing Sarah Brindle? The theatre was up ahead. Would JP still be there? The double doors at the front the building opened. There he was. JP *was* there. He was standing at the top of the steps. There was something wrong. He was holding his hand up to his chest. He was hurt. Terribly hurt. I could see it at once. *Mrs R has got here before me.* I ran up the steps and put an arm around JP. He looked at me, grabbed at my hand, and then collapsed, blood pooling at our feet.

26

I waited by JP's bedside for two days. The doctors told me I had to go home, that they would bring me news when there was any, but that it was too early to determine the outcome. He had been stabbed twice, once in the chest and once in the back, and the injuries were severe. The surgeons had operated on him and he was unconscious and needed recuperation and rest. Eventually, I accepted, reluctantly, that I needed rest myself, and food, and so I returned to my rooms. I also remembered about poor Moll. JP's dear dog, Moll. After a little bit of persuasion, the doorman at Rogerson Court let me into his room and there she was, tired and a bit anxious but wagging her tail. I told her I would look after her until her master was better. It was the least I could do.

Obviously, my strongest emotion in those early hours was concern for my friend, but I was consumed with guilt too. Why hadn't I realised sooner the truth about Mrs R? Why hadn't I learned my lesson and gone to JP first and told him about my suspicions? We could've gone to Mrs R together or told the police together. Instead – pig-headed idiot that I am – I insisted on going to see Mrs R on my own and aroused her anger and passion – all the emotions that we'd seen glimpses of before, beneath the veneer, and she'd met JP at the theatre and stabbed him. And what else could I think? *It was my fault.*

Of course, as soon as I realised JP had been attacked, and as soon as we'd got him to hospital, I overcame my reluctance about going to the police at once, and went to the station and told them everything about my encounter with Mrs R. A couple of constables were sent to her house but she'd gone. *Of course she'd gone.* Her neighbours said she'd had left earlier that day with two packing cases and no, she hadn't left a forwarding address. But perhaps the greater shock, which I learned shortly afterwards, was that Gray was gone too. I discovered it when I went to tell him JP had been attacked. There was no one at his apartment and there was no one there the following day either. And I think I knew straightaway why. Mrs R had shown a fierce loyalty to her son and now it was his turn to return the favour and show loyalty to her, and he would. Mrs R was attempting to escape justice and her son had gone with her.

I returned to the hospital on the third day to discover JP was still unconscious and so I sat outside in the waiting area and walked around the grounds of the hospital smoking cigarettes and put the same questions to the same doctors with the same answers. Mrs R was constantly on my mind too. Why hadn't I seen it before? I'd seen for myself the intensity of her love for Gray and its twin emotion – her hatred for the drugs that had enslaved him – but I could think of another word for her love now: *obsessive.* Gray had ended the relationship with Sarah Brindle and they'd remained friends, but that would've been too much for Mrs R. Had the mother become jealous of the woman who loved her son? I lit a cigarette and continued my tense walk around the hospital grounds.

There were a couple of things that stopped me from going completely mad. Firstly, JP's loyal little mongrel Moll was a great comfort and, when I rested my hand on her soft head, she seemed like a connection to my friend. Secondly, there were regular visits from Elizabeth Mackie, the nurse, who would drop in when she was working in the hospital and sit with me and listen patiently as I talked about my suspicions about Mrs R. I could see the look on her face though, and I'd think: *you don't believe me, do you?* There were also visits from Dan and Rachel and Barbara, and I also got to meet JP's parents for the first time. They appeared to be his only family; they were certainly the only relatives who visited. God forgive me, but when I saw them both – a man who'd obviously been physically strong once and a much smaller woman who barely spoke – my first thought was what Mrs R had told me: how JP's father had *beaten* him and how his mother had come between them. It didn't seem possible now: JP's father looked so withered and weak. I also remembered a letter in which JP told me about the effects his parents had had on him. I dug it out one evening after I'd returned from the hospital and read it again and there it was: *My parents taught me how to be silent.*

Reading and re-reading JP's letters offered some distraction in those early days. I would also go into the hospital as much as I could and sit by JP's bed when the doctors allowed me to. His chest was heavily bandaged, and his face deadly white. But he was breathing. Up down. Up down. Occasionally, he would open his eyes for a second or two, then close them again. Otherwise, he lay perfectly still and nothing seemed to disturb his sleep, not even the nurses turning him over or changing his bandages. Occasionally, I would say something to him with no certainty that he could hear me – at first, just the odd word of friendship and loyalty which slowly became longer speeches about what we'd been through. In the quiet of the hospital ward, I even told him about my visit to Mrs R and apologised to him for not consulting him. And JP would sleep on and, eventually, I would go home and try to sleep myself.

As to the search for Mrs R, I heard nothing from the police after their initial visit to her house, so I eventually went to the station myself to find out what was happening.

It took considerable courage to go there, I must say. I still remembered my first encounter with Chief Inspector Downs and him leaning across to me and hissing that word in my ear ... *coward*. But I owed it to JP to find out what was going on and so I screwed my courage to the sticking place and went down to the station anyway. As it happened, the dreaded Chief Inspector Downs was not there that day, and his assistant was much less threatening (perhaps he hadn't seen my papers). But he said the investigation was continuing and that nothing had been heard, or seen, of Mrs R or her son. I was told we would have to wait for Mr Allgood to recover – *if he recovered* – before anything more could be done.

And so my vigil continued. Sometimes, I would go to the library and sit in front of my books and read the same sentence repeatedly without taking any of it in, but mostly I trudged between my rooms and the hospital. On the fifth day, one of the nurses told me JP had opened his eyes for quite some time but hadn't said anything and I reminded her of something which I'd told the staff many times before: of course JP didn't say anything. JP doesn't say anything. He never says anything, and the nurse nodded without appearing to take it again and told me to get some rest myself. But instead, I sat in the waiting room and smoked a cigarette and then another one and another one. I would often go over the last few months as I sat there. My first encounter with JP. That feeling I'd had that we should be friends and would be. The note he'd passed me – *someone is trying to kill me* – and where it had taken us. And I'd sit there and think: JP is as dear to me as he could possibly be. He mustn't die. He mustn't.

It was on the sixth day that JP started to show some signs of improvement. He began to open his eyes for longer periods, minutes at a time, and I could see some of the colour returning to his face. The doctors also seemed more optimistic and said he might well be over the worst. During one of our visits, Elizabeth Mackie asked me if I'd dared to hope that when JP recovered, he might be *completely* recovered. 'Do you mean able to talk again?' I said, and she nodded. It hadn't even crossed my mind. I'd become so used to my silent friend, I was so familiar with his ways and communicating by letter and scribbled note, that there was part of me that had grown to rather cherish it. We had built up a friendship and intimacy even though I'd never heard him talk, and now Miss Mackie had suggested that perhaps he might. He might wake up and *speak to me.*

But there was no such miracle, only slow steady progress with JP opening his eyes for longer and longer each day. He was still terribly weak. One of the doctors told me JP had been stabbed in the chest with considerable force, in the left pleural cavity, and was lucky to be alive, and when he said it, the first thing I saw in my mind's eye were those pale, thin hands of Mrs R. Hands picking at the lace of her neck, and writing that threatening letter, and picking up a knife and driving it into JP's chest, and I could feel the anger rising in me again and I would think: when JP gets better, we will find her. *We will find Mrs R.*

Then, as I paced the hospital grounds or walked through the streets with Moll, the anger would be replaced by despondency that JP might not get better which in turn would be replaced by hope that he would. And that's what those days were like. I would occasionally have awkward conversations with JP's parents in the hospital waiting room – he hadn't seen them for months before he was attacked – and Miss Mackie and I would comfort each other with cigarettes and strong tea in the hospital canteen. But mostly it was just JP and I, him lying flat in his bed, me sitting on the chair by his side, together in our familiar silence.

The breakthrough came at the end of the first week. For seven full days, JP had shown no real signs of change, other than occasionally opening his eyes, but on the seventh day he began to move his arms. Occasionally, he would put a hand up to his mouth and we came to realise this meant he wanted water. On other occasions, his fingers would pull at the bedclothes, anxiously. Later, when his strength seemed to be returning even more, he put his hand out until he found mine and, weakly at first, then with more power, he held my hand in his until he drifted off to sleep again and his hand went slack.

The following day, JP seemed a little stronger still and, when I went in to see him, he seemed agitated about something. He signalled with his hand and I asked him if it was water, or food, he wanted, or a nurse, and, very slowly, he shook his head. Eventually, he made his meaning known. He wanted something from the cupboard by his bed. I opened it and looked inside. His book and pen. I held it up for him. 'You want this?' I asked and his eyes brightened. I put the book down on his bed. Did he have the strength to write anything? He reached out towards the book, then seemed to collapse back on the pillow. Every movement still required an immense amount of energy. But he was determined.

I opened the book at a fresh page and handed him the pen. He could barely hold it. His fingers were limp, but with a little help from me, supporting his hand from beneath, he began to write. His eyes never left the page.

The first word emerged. Slowly.

Mrs

He stopped for a second, then continued.

Mrs R

He'd heard me! He'd heard me talking about her at his bedside and he'd understood. He seemed to be gathering his strength to continue.

is not the killer

I leaned over JP's bed. 'No JP,' I said. 'I *know*. I went to see her. She's the one who wrote the letters and pushed you under the car. And she must have killed Sarah too.'

JP looked at me and seemed to be gathering his strength again for one more push. His chest heaved. Then slowly, he reached out for the paper again. I felt a sudden sense of guilt. I shouldn't be putting him through this. I told him he should rest, he was straining himself, but he squeezed my hand and the meaning was obvious. He wanted to write something else.

Another word.

the

His hand slipped but then he continued.

killer is

His writing was becoming fainter as his hand was becoming weaker. His breathing was becoming laboured. I could feel my own breathing. I held his hand up so he could carry on. The pen was slack in his hand, but then, with a final effort, before he collapsed back on the bed unconscious, he wrote one last word.

Gray.

27

The first thing I did was call for a nurse. I told her JP had slipped into unconsciousness again and she came to the bedside and took his pulse and his temperature and said he was fine, but he must be left alone to sleep and that I should wait outside in the corridor. It was a relief that he was OK. My worry was that the huge effort JP had made to write the note had been too much for him. *The note.* Perhaps JP had mis-heard me, or misunderstood me, when I'd told him Mrs R was the killer. But his words were clear. I looked at the notebook. I'd taken it out with me to the corridor. Up ahead, the nurse's shoes were clacking loudly on the wooden floor. I sat down on the chair by the door to the ward. Once again, my emotions, thoughts, were unclear. *The killer is Gray.* There it was. Four words, each lighter and weaker than the one before as JP's energy deserted him. *The killer is Gray.* How? How could the killer be Gray? Gray had been standing *next to JP* when Sarah Brindle was stabbed. It couldn't be Gray. It was impossible. *The killer is Gray.*

I turned the pages of the notebook. It was a record of all the little messages he'd scribbled to me, and others, over the last few months. *Someone tried to push me in front of a motor car. I miss Gray desperately. Why did they throw the mask out of the window? It's about what I can't remember.* I kept turning the pages, backwards through the scraps of the last few months until I reached the front of the book and there, on the first page, was the old rhyme. Again. Always the old rhyme. One line was underlined, and then underlined again. *Tell me what you see, lad, tell me what you see.*

I realised I was exhausted. I closed the book and rested my head back on the wall behind me. For days now, my life had been one long crisis. The confrontation with Mrs R. JP on the stairs of the theatre, bleeding. The disappearance of Mrs R, and Gray. JP in hospital, weak and frail under the bandages. Then his hand, scraping out the words on the book. *The killer is Gray.* I would go to the police now, I thought. I would go to the police right now and show them the book and tell them … what could I tell them? I didn't know why JP had written the note. I had no evidence against Gray. I didn't even believe that Gray killed Sarah Brindle. And no one knew where he was. I felt a desperation to *do something* and a realisation that there was nothing I could do except wait for JP to recover. I looked in on JP one more time, put the notebook on the bedside table, and went back to my rooms.

The following day, I returned to the hospital early (there was no change in JP), then went to the library and did some reading (without really concentrating), then went back to the hospital again in the afternoon, to find that JP had slept through it all. The day after that, however, there was some noticeable improvement in his condition. When I arrived, JP's eyes were open and he'd been slightly propped up by the nurses. I couldn't hide my relief. I also desperately wanted to ask him about the note – *the killer is Gray* – but I could see that he was still weak. Instead, I sat quietly by his bedside and watched the nurses come and go and occasionally JP and I would look at each other and, for the first time I think since JP had been taken to hospital, I began to feel that things might be OK. I could feel my fear for him – the fear that he might not recover, that he might die – starting to fade. I could see him getting stronger. I could see him getting better.

I finally asked him about the note the following day,

when I could see he was starting to regain his strength more rapidly. I took the notebook from the table and showed it to him, and he nodded, then raised his hand. He was looking for a pen. I took one out of my jacket and handed it to him and he wrote a message. He was still weak but getting stronger. The message read: *give me time*. I put the book on his bedside table and said of course I would give him time. It also struck me then that Elizabeth Mackie had been wrong: it looked like JP would recover from this terrible attack, but he would not recover *completely*. I asked him if he wanted me to go to the police, but he shook his head, squeezed my hand, closed his eyes and went to sleep.

In the days that followed, I could see JP recovering more and more of his physical strength. By the end of the second week, he was sitting up in bed and eating by myself, and I could see he had also struck up a strong bond with the nurses. They were bewildered, of course, by the fact JP didn't, or couldn't, speak. And I remember one of the nurses, a chatty Scottish girl, asking me lots of questions about JP and why he was silent, and what might have caused his condition. And I told her everything I knew, which was very little. She supposed it must have been the war, she said, and leaned it closer to me and said two words: *shell shock*. I also, as gently as I could, brought JP round to the subject of our investigations. I told him every detail of my confrontation with Mrs R, and he listened carefully. I also began to press him to tell me what he meant by his note, the note that Gray was the killer, and he would reach for the bits of paper by the side of his bed and scratch out little messages. He told me that he meant what he said, Gray was the killer, and that he'd written the message to me as soon as he'd been able to because he was afraid he was about to die. He also wrote an appeal for me to be patient and wait for him to fully regain his strength and then, he promised, he would put everything down on paper.

Eventually, much to my frustration, I decided I would simply have to wait until JP was ready. I watched him get better. I watched him move from the bed to a wheelchair and from there to his feet, although he could only walk with a stick. His writing also became stronger, and he would write me notes saying he had been ordering his thoughts and was almost ready to write it all down. And, in another of his messages, he said he knew it was frustrating for me, but he had to get it all straight in his own head first. He wasn't even sure if he was right. The truth – or what he thought was the truth – had always been there, he wrote, but it had been in pieces, and he had to get the pieces in the right order. *Please be patient my friend,* he wrote, *I will tell you everything soon.*

It was a week or so later that the moment finally came. I'd gone into the ward as usual in the morning and when I arrived, JP was standing by the window. He was leaning a little on his stick but I could see that he needed it less and less each day. When he heard me, he turned round and I noticed he had something in his other hand. It was some paper. Several pages. I knew right away what it was. He held the sheets of paper out to me and I took them and glanced at the first line. *Dear Harry, this is the truth as far as I know it.* I asked him if I could read it right away and he nodded and so I went out into the corridor, sat on the chair by the door, and started reading. There follows an exact account of what the letter said.

Dear Harry,

This is the truth as far as I know it. The killer is Gray. What I have told you a hundred times, and what my own memory tells me, is that Gray was standing next to me as Sarah Brindle was stabbed, but what I now believe is that Sarah Brindle was stabbed to death by Gray. I have spent the last few weeks here in my hospital bed trying to order my thoughts, trying to arrange the pieces of the truth – and thank you, dear Harry, for being patient while I did so. I now think I have my thoughts in order. I now think I can tell you the truth.

You know already that there were various questions that bothered us about Sarah's murder. Why the murderer wore a gown. Why he wore a mask. Why Sarah's screams sounded *odd*. Do you remember Rachel telling us that, in the cafe? She said the screams sounded strange and she thought they might be connected to a play. And you know that various other thoughts – the same thoughts – kept occurring to me. *Something wasn't there.* And the nursery rhyme. It was always on my mind. It led us to Gray. *What's at the top of the stairs?* But I always felt it had more to reveal. *Tell me what you see, lad, tell me what you see.* Then there was everything the doctors were telling me about my memories and how they worked and how they didn't work: the way in which we remember, but also how we can *un*-remember, and *mis*-remember. All of it felt important, always, but for a long time, I wasn't sure why.

And none of it led me to suspect Gray anyway. That began in a different way. Do you remember him telling us he was being watched? Do you remember he said he could sometimes see a man standing back in the trees, or walking up and down the street, and he was worried it might be one of the men he owed money to, from the old days, or even the man who killed Sarah? I was worried for Gray when he told me that, but he said he couldn't go to the police because it would mean coming out of hiding and exposing his mother to possible arrest or shame. And so I decided I would take action myself. I would keep a watch on the watcher. I went into the pub on the corner of Gray's street and I wrote a little letter for the publican explaining that I couldn't speak because of an injury I'd sustained in the war and I told him that all I wanted to do was sit in his window and drink beer, so that's what I did, for hours on end, and days on end. I sat there and kept a watch on Gray's street.

For days, nothing happened – I ordered beer and nothing happened – but it was that vigil in the pub that alerted me to the first piece of the truth. I did not tell Gray what I was doing. I did not tell you either. I did not want either of you to worry about me or try to convince me I should stop. I sincerely believed I was doing the right thing, that I was protecting my friend. But then something odd happened. During one of our walks round the park, Gray told me that the stranger had been in his street again, walking up and down for two hours, keeping watch on the apartment. But I knew that could not be so, for I was in the pub keeping watch on the same day. I had kept a watch on the street for the entire afternoon and evening. So I knew that there had been no man walking up and down the street when Gray said there was. *I knew Gray was lying.*

That was the first time that I began to doubt my old friend and, even though I loved Gray dearly, and hoped, a long time ago, that he might love me back, I asked myself: what else might be a lie, what else might be untrue? At first, I wanted to challenge him about it, to demand that he explain why he was lying about the stranger in the street, but then an instinct told me to tell Gray nothing. I sometimes wonder why I had that instinct. Perhaps, without me being prepared to admit it, something made me suspicious of Gray *before* I began the vigil in the pub.

I then thought back over what Gray had told me and tried

to apply a test to everything he'd said and ask whether it was true or false. He told us – he told everyone – that it was he who had ended his affair with Sarah but perhaps it was the other way around; perhaps it was Sarah who ended the affair but allowed Gray to tell everyone something different. That would be just like dear, kind Sarah. She wouldn't have minded giving Gray the dignity of telling people it was *he* who ended the affair. And what if there were other lies too? What if there were lies about the day of the murder itself? At first, I could barely believe it. I *knew* the facts about the murder. I had heard them from many people many times. *I was there.* A man in a gown and mask was crouched over Sarah's body. Gray screamed 'they're stabbing Sarah'. The murderer slammed the door shut and I ran to get the police while Gray tried to kick the door in. But what if some of that was a lie? What if those words were a lie: 'they're stabbing Sarah.' *What if it was all a lie?*

Forgive me Harry. I think I will have to stop this letter for now. It is taking rather more out of me than I anticipated. My wrist hurts, and my head hurts a little too. I think I should rest now. I will continue tomorrow.

10am

Dear Harry,

I did the right thing resting last night, I think. The nurses keep telling me I must stop sitting up in bed writing long letters. I'm sure they're right, and my energy certainly ebbs and flows. The pain in my chest is also most intense sometimes. But I have had a long time to get my thoughts in order and I must get them down on paper. I will resume my account and continue for as long as I can.

As I told you, I had begun to question what Gray had been saying to me – what was true and what was false – and it was around the same time, fortuitously, that I again started to attend the military hospital, St Clare's, and came under the treatment of Hearns – the brilliant Dr Hearns. As you know, Hearns believed the key to my condition was memory and for days I seemed to write down all the memories I'd ever had. My childhood, parents, my friendship with Gray, Sarah's murder, right up to my time at the Front. Hearns wanted to know everything about my years in France. The friends I made. The friends I lost. *The memories I would rather forget.* He said it was the key to everything. He said he could help me to forget.

I must admit, I was sceptical, but Hearns told me how the process might work. It relied on prolonged periods of deep hypnosis, he said, and was based on several established principles of memory. Not all memories are true, he told me. Memories can be highly unreliable. One can remember events that didn't happen or didn't happen in the way one thought they did. And memories can be edited and *adjusted*, he said. Sometimes, the brain does the editing and adjusting itself – our subconscious forgets and remembers a thousand things every day – but sometimes the adjustment is done by *other people,* and this is what he hoped he would be able to do to me under hypnosis. Our memories, he said, can be influenced and shaped, for good or ill. We may even form memories based on what other people tell us and come to believe they are our own memories. This was common, Hearns told me, in conditions of high stress or fear, when memories can be highly unreliable and suggestable. The trenches in France for example. *Or the scene of a murder.*

The potential implications of what Hearns was saying didn't strike me instantly but I started to apply what Dr

Hearns had told me to my own experiences. I already knew that some of what Gray told me was untrue, but I wondered if my own memories could also be unreliable. As you know, in the days and weeks after we discovered Gray in hiding, he went over the story of the day Sarah was killed, again and again, and I began to think about what he actually said. And that's when I noticed something strange: Gray's memory was working the *wrong way*. As time goes by, our memories fade, the details blur, but the opposite seemed to be happening with Gray. The more he talked about the day Sarah died, the clearer his memory seemed to become, the more the details seemed to come into focus, and I realised, or supposed, that it was happening that way because it wasn't really a memory, or at least it wasn't a real memory, and he'd been doing it from the beginning. Gray wasn't remembering how Sarah died, he was writing a story and he had been from the moment she was murdered: the story of something that never happened.

It was Dr Hearns who made me see all of this. He told me that memories can be unreliable and we can even form memories based on what *other people* have told us happened. Is that what had happened to me? I wrote to Hearns about it, I told him the whole story, and he said the only way to get to the truth – *the real memory* – was to eliminate everything that people tell you and everything you've read and all the impressions from other sources – pictures, photographs, letters – eliminate it all and focus instead on what you actually saw. *Tell me what you see, lad, tell me what you see.*

And that's when I really started to realise, Harry. Do you remember I wrote a note to you: *something wasn't there.* And so I tried to do what Dr Hearns told me to do. I tried to forget everything except what I *saw* and *knew*. I thought back to the night at the theatre. We heard the screams. We ran up the stairs. We saw Sarah being stabbed by a man, or person, wearing a gown and mask. The door was slammed in our faces. I ran downstairs while Gray attempted to kick the door in. The police arrived and broke the door down and Sarah was there. Sarah had been murdered. She had been stabbed to death.

But how much of that did I *see* and *know*, how much of it was *my memory*? I definitely heard the screams, but did I *know* that they were the screams of Sarah being attacked? Gray definitely told me that he had been attempting to kick the door down while I was away fetching the police, but did I *know* he had done that? And I definitely believed that I saw a man crouching over Sarah and stabbing her to death. But was that really another fact that I knew? The words of Dr Hearns came to mind again: *we can even form memories based on what other people have told us happened.* I realised, Harry. I realised how wrong I'd been, how deceived, deluded. Something wasn't there. *Sarah wasn't there.*

Oh Harry, I am so tired and the nurse has just told me I must rest. I will sleep for a little while, and return.

3.30pm

Dear Harry,

I slept for a few hours and feel much better, I must admit, although I am still so weak at times. There is still the pain in my chest, but the nurse has given me my pills so I feel able to return to these pages. I will finish the story now and then I can rest for as long as I need.

So, I was realising, piece by piece, thanks to Dr Hearns, how my memory had cheated me. What Hearns told me is that memories can be locked down into the subconscious and that an event, or another memory, can suddenly unlock them. I also realised what Gray had done to me. He had done precisely what Dr Hearns said could be done: he had told me what happened and I had taken it on as my own memory and he had started as soon as we got to the top of the stairs. 'They're stabbing Sarah,' he said and, when the door was closed, he kept saying it. 'Someone was stabbing Sarah.' 'Sarah has been stabbed.' He was telling me what had happened, he was telling me what I'd seen, and it became my own memory. Remember what Dr Hearns said. In conditions of high stress or fear, memories can be highly unreliable and suggestable. And Gray went on doing it, even after we discovered him in hiding. He kept telling the story, adding little details, making sure that I still remembered what he was telling me to remember.

Let me tell you about the shame I felt. Let me tell you what a fool I felt. I told the police what I'd seen at the theatre. I told you, I told everyone what I thought happened the day Sarah was murdered, but all the time I was nothing but an idiot, a weak-minded, suggestible idiot. I had been *told* what had happened by Gray. I had been led and influenced. I wrote to Dr Hearns again and he tried to reassure me. If it was true, there was nothing to be ashamed of, he said, everyone's memories are made up of memories that are true and memories that we believe to be true. And when I thought about it, I could see how it worked. I could see that my *false memory* – that I had *seen* Sarah being stabbed to death – was reinforced by my *true* memory, that she was stabbed to death. I saw her body.

So what did I actually see when the door was open for those few seconds? This is only a theory Harry, but it is a theory which I think is confirmed by the wound in the side of my chest, a wound inflicted by my former friend Gray.

What I think I actually saw that day is this. We heard screams. We ran up the stairs. The door was open. *Someone* was crouching down on the floor with his back to us, the knife held in the air. It was at that point that Gray shouted 'they're stabbing Sarah!' but what I actually saw was a figure, in a gown and a mask, holding a knife in the air. I saw the figure in the gown. But *I didn't see Sarah.* Sarah wasn't there.

What really happened? I don't know for certain, but here is the rest of my theory. I put it together from the bits and pieces and my plan was to put it all to Gray at the theatre before he inflicted the wound that's throbbing under this bandage. First, I thought about the screams. Rachel said they sounded odd and, at first, she thought they might have been from a play, an actress rehearsing, pretending. Rachel then realised later that Sarah had been murdered and assumed she'd heard Sarah's dying screams. But surely Dr Hearns's theories could apply here too. Memories are distorted and changed to incorporate new information. Rachel initially thought the screams were odd and sounded pretend, but then adjusted her impression to fit the facts that she learned later on. But maybe she'd been right the first time. Maybe the screams weren't real. What if Sarah *had been pretending*?

I have to admit, my theorising stalled here for some time Harry. Why on earth, I said to myself, would Sarah pretend to scream just before she was murdered? It made no sense. And I remembered what Barbara said, that day when we were sitting in her café and she was talking about Gray and telling us how much he loved practical jokes – he put a dead mouse in her desk, do you remember? What if Sarah had pretended to scream because she thought it was all a practical joke?

I could then see how it might have worked. Gray told

Sarah 'Let's play a practical joke on JP. You scream, and JP and I will run upstairs and it will look like there's been a murder.' He probably showed her the mask and gown. The plan was that she would put them on, pose as the murderer, slam the door shut and lock it, and poor JP would think it was real, and then Gray would reveal the joke and they'd all have a big laugh about it. And so that's what happened. The signal for the joke was when Gray and I arrived at the theatre and started coming upstairs. Sarah put the mask and gown on. She screamed. She went down on the floor as if she was crouching over someone, posing as the murderer, with her back to the door. Gray shouted 'they're stabbing Sarah' and Sarah slammed the door shut. And Gray told me to run downstairs and fetch the police.

Now, Sarah thought she knew what was going to happen next. Gray was going to open the door and wait for me to come back and the practical joke would be revealed. I can't imagine how much convincing Sarah needed to take part. She was an actress; perhaps she thought it was fun. Perhaps she was simply indulging Gray like she'd indulged his practical jokes in the past. Or perhaps she went along with it because she had seen his reaction when she told him their relationship was over and she was a little *afraid* of him when he didn't get his way, when she said no to him.

She was right to be afraid, because Gray had it planned out. There was no practical joke. As soon as I ran downstairs, he asked Sarah to open the door. He told her to take off the gown and mask, quick. Then he pulled out a knife he had hidden in his coat and stabbed her. Again and again, until she was dead. He stuffed the gown in the box of costumes. He threw the mask out of the window – he wanted to create the impression that the killer had run away from the theatre and discarded the mask on the way.

He didn't want anyone to suspect that the killer had been in the theatre all the time and still was. It was one of the reasons the mask didn't make sense. The 'killer' I saw had to wear a mask because I couldn't be allowed to know that it *wasn't who it was supposed to be* – that it was Sarah.

I don't know if every part of this theory is true, but all the parts seem to fit together. I suppose that once he'd killed Sarah, he concealed the knife in his jacket again, he left the room, locked the door and concealed the key. Perhaps there was blood on him, but I remembered something else: when the police and I got to the top of the stairs, Gray was crouched down in a ball, crying, and when the police kicked in the door, he rushed in and picked Sarah's body up and held her in his arms. And I realised, when I thought about it, why he might have done that: there may have been spots of Sarah's blood on him and he concealed that fact by crouching down and then he held Sarah as soon as he could so any blood on him would not be suspicious.

What do you think Harry? I am getting tired again now, but you must tell me what you think of my theory. I can imagine Mrs R worrying, when I first start asking questions, that I was getting to the truth and pushing me under the car and then putting that note under your door. Which leaves just one last part of it to go, the one that ended with the knife in my chest. I was stupid again, I'm afraid. I decided that I would meet Gray at the theatre and put my theory to him; I also wanted to look at the scene of the crime again and judge whether my theory felt right. And I hope that my meeting with Gray would go well. Perhaps our long friendship would mean something, perhaps he would be honest or *perhaps* my theory was wrong, perhaps there was some other explanation for what happened to Sarah Brindle. But Gray had come prepared.

Before I knew what was happening, he stabbed me, then fled. What a macabre circle: that I should end up stabbed in the same room as Sarah.

I must stop now Harry. My hand is so weak, I can barely write these last few words. I'm going to rest and when I see you next, I'm going to give you these pages to read. I have no idea what you will make of them. I have no idea if they are true. But it is my theory. It is what I believe happened to my good friend Sarah Brindle.

With all my trust and affection,

JP.

28

I'm not certain how long I sat there, in the hospital corridor, after I'd read JP's letter. But I do remember that, as soon as I'd finished reading it, I went back to the start and read it again, then again. I had no idea what to make of it or whether JP could be right. How did it fit in with what I knew, or suspected, about Mrs R? Why had JP not taken me into his confidence? Why had I not taken JP into mine? I was tired and bewildered, unable to move. Perhaps I would never move again. Perhaps I would sit here, on this little chair in the corridor of a county hospital, forever.

It was one of the nurses who broke into my brown study. She tapped me on the shoulder and indicated the door to the ward. 'I think Mr Allgood would like to see you,' she said. I looked up. JP was standing by the door, looking at me, concerned. How vulnerable he appeared, suddenly. The bandages round his chest. The hand holding on to the stick, knuckles white. I got up and started to offer my support, putting my hand under his arm, but he waved me away gently and walked back to his bed. I could see that, in fact, he was getting stronger all the time.

I followed him, saw him into bed, then sat down on the chair by the side. I put his letter, his theory, on the bedsheet and told him I didn't know what to make of it. I told him I didn't know if it was a work of logic or fantasy, medicine or imagination, detection or fiction. JP leaned forward and pointed to the first line: *this is the truth as far as I know it.* Of course, if it was true, it would explain why Gray and Mrs R had disappeared. I had assumed Mrs R was the culprit and Gray was the loyal son, but it could be the other way round: Gray as the murderer and Mrs R his loyal mother. And it made sense. I knew already what Mrs R was prepared to do to protect her son, and I felt certain she would also try to protect him from the gallows if he was a murderer. Was JP right? Had my friend done what he'd always wanted to do: arranged the pieces of the truth in the proper order? Right or wrong, the police needed to know. I told JP I wanted to take the letter to Chief Inspector Downs right away. We had to find Gray and Mrs R at once and establish the truth of the matter. JP looked wary at first. His hand reached out to the letter as if he might pull it back to him. Then he put his head to one side and closed his eyes. He needed to sleep. I picked up the letter, folded it, put it in my pocket, and left.

When I visited the police station later and gave JP's letter to Chief Inspector Downs, his reaction, after he'd read it, was entirely the one I expected. As usual, the chief inspector could not conceal his personal contempt for me, but I could see that he didn't give much credence to JP's letter either. He told me his officers would begin the necessary investigations. I became a little angry at that, I must admit. I told him my friend was lying in a hospital bed recovering from terrible stab wounds and that he had almost died and the culprits were still at large. The chief inspector told me he was fully aware of the circumstances and that Mrs R and her son *would be found*. In the meantime, he suggested I should go home and rest. *Not that again*. I do wish people would stop telling me to get some rest.

In the days that followed, I continued to wrestle with my thoughts and doubts, and the extent to which I believed, or dis-believed, JP's letter, and when it all became too much for me, alone in my rooms, I would take Moll out for long walks round the park and down by the riverside, and it helped a little. But I always found that, when I got back to my rooms, the questions were waiting for me. If Gray killed Sarah Brindle, *why* had he done it? And could memories really be created and distorted in the way JP described? I thought about what Mrs R said: she told us she had seen her son's body in the morgue, she told us she buried him and wept at his graveside, and we believed her because it is the human instinct: we believe what people tell us unless we have evidence to the contrary. And Gray did the same thing. He said Sarah Brindle was lying on the floor of the theatre. He said someone was stabbing her. He said he was being followed and that a stranger was watching his apartment. And so, lies become truth.

I kept up my visits to JP, of course, and in the week after he'd given me the letter, he continued to improve every single day. I asked him once if he thought his time in hospital had changed him, and what I meant by that, without saying it directly, was whether my friend was now closer – or further away – from one day regaining his speech. JP grasped my meaning straight away and pushed his notebook and pen to one side. A look came over his face, an intense look which I had occasionally seen before, that made me think that he was about to *say something*. He opened his mouth and narrowed his eyes. His hands curled into fists. It was as if a word had formed in his mind and he was now trying to force it from his body. But then the moment passed. His mouth closed. His fists uncurled. And he put his head back on his pillow, exhausted.

A week or so later, the doctors finally told JP he was ready to leave hospital. His parents had tried to convince him he should go back to the family home with them, but he wrote an anxious little note to me that it was the last thing he wanted and so I arranged to help him move back into his rooms. He was delighted, most of all, to see Moll and the feeling was mutual. When we arrived at his rooms, before I could stop her, the dog jumped up at her master and JP winced in pain as she thudded into his leg. But he quickly recovered and clearly held nothing against his beloved mongrel. They were delighted to see each other. I made sure JP had everything he needed.

My life then settled in a bizarre little routine again. I would drop into JP's rooms three times a day to make sure he was feeling fine, and to walk Moll, and then I would go up to the university and spend a few hours every day with my books. Occasionally – *often* – I'd find that my mind had wandered from British history to the many questions posed by my adventures with JP. Often, I would wonder *why* I had gone to see Mrs R on my own and *why* JP had done the same thing and not confided in me about his suspicions over Gray. At first, I admit, I felt a little angry with him. I felt that he'd *left me out.* But the more I thought about it, the more I realised, I think, that both of us, JP and I, had grown closer than we'd realised. We were motivated, particularly JP, by the desire to discover the truth about who murdered Sarah Brindle, but, as time passed, I think we were also motivated by the desire to impress each other, and please each other. And protect each other. I couldn't feel angry with JP. I was just pleased he was alive.

I was also keen to encourage his rehabilitation and so, about a week after he returned to his rooms, I encouraged him to take his first walk outside. At first, he was cautious but once we were out and JP could see that it was a beautiful day, he rather enjoyed himself. Moll scampered round like a puppy, looking for unfeasibly large sticks and dropping them at her master's feet for him to throw even though JP couldn't bend down yet. I think we must have walked for around 15 minutes or so and I felt that, after an extraordinary few weeks, it was a little glimpse of normality. A sign of hope.

My mood changed as soon as I got back to my rooms. I had proposed to write to Chief Inspector Downs again and ask him whether there had been any progress in his investigations (I was not hopeful). But as I arrived back at my rooms, I realised I was rather tired and would probably have an early night. As I opened the door, I was imagining a cup of hot tea and some toast and then bed, which is when I noticed the piece of paper on the floor. It had been pushed under the door. I felt the sudden grip of anxiety: I remembered what had happened before. But I tried to reassure myself as I bent down to pick it up. It was probably just a letter from my landlady or one of the other students who lived in the building. I opened the note and read it and the anxiety and fear came rushing back. I could feel the blood in my veins. The words were the same as before. *WE KILLED SARAH BRINDLE AND WE WILL KILL YOU TOO.*

I went over to my bed and sat down, my legs shaking. Could this be the *same* letter, the one I'd given to the police? Had it somehow ended up back in my rooms? Was that possible? I went to my desk and opened the drawer. No. Someone had crept up the stairs and pushed *another* letter under my door. And I could see now, looking at the new letter more closely, that it was slightly different. It used the same capital letters, but it was a different hand. *Gray*. He was here. Somewhere close. I remembered Gray telling me how he and his mother had talked about going abroad to live and I'd assumed, after the attack on JP, that they had gone ahead with their plan and were now in another country. But the letter told me something else. They were close by, and watching, and probably willing to kill again.

The following morning, I took the letter to the police

straight away and, when I showed it to them, I think I detected, at last, a shift in their attitude. Perhaps they were finally beginning to take the situation seriously. JP, on the other hand, was rather calm when I told him. He asked for his notebook and wrote a note to the effect that he had expected two things: either to never hear from Gray and Mrs R again, or to discover that Gray was determined to *finish the job.* He'd killed Sarah Brindle and stabbed JP and perhaps he would try to kill JP again and try to kill me too. I went back to the station and told the Chief Inspector that JP needed the protection of the police immediately, but Downs trotted out the usual cliches of the constabulary: everything was under control, he said.

The second letter came a couple of days later and was sent to JP. He showed it to me when I arrived in the morning to accompany him on his now daily walk in the park. *The Day of the Lord will come like a thief,* it said. The day after, there was another. *Those who reject me and do not accept my message have one who will judge them.* There appeared to be no attempt to disguise the handwriting this time. JP showed me some old letters from Gray. The writing was the same. Every couple of days after that, there was another message, always a quotation from the Bible, usually on a theme of vengeance. *God did not spare the angels who sinned, but threw them into hell, where they are kept chained in darkness.* And another: *She had a hard and stubborn heart that made her punishment even greater.* Gray was obviously threatening us, but it seemed to me that, in his dark, perverse way, he was also explaining what he'd done. *She had a hard and stubborn heart.* He meant Sarah.

After about two weeks or so, the letters stopped, but rather than take it as a sign that perhaps Gray had given up, JP was suddenly struck by another idea. He explained it in a letter he wrote to me from his rooms and I was extremely reluctant at first. JP still hadn't fully recovered his strength and I thought he should be protecting himself rather than putting himself back in the line of danger. And Gray was dangerous. But, when I objected, JP wrote me another letter telling me that, if I was unwilling to help, he would go ahead and do it himself. Which left me no choice.

We executed the plan the next day and the landlord of the pub recognised JP straight away and showed him to the seat by the window. JP sat back in his chair with his head resting back on the wall to reduce the possibility of being seen from the street. I sat next to him, a little further back, giving me a clear view of Gray's apartment. But it seemed unlikely to me that Gray would return. Surely, he and his mother would have flown the country by now. JP wasn't so certain: in his letter, he'd reminded me that we were dealing with someone who was cunning – his manipulation of the events of Sarah's murder proved that – but also *not normal*.

On the first day, there was no sign. The same the second day. By the third, I was beginning to doubt the wisdom of the enterprise, but JP wouldn't budge. He would sip his watered-down beer, keep his eyes fixed on the street, and then, when his beer was finished, order another. And so I made a promise to myself, a little reluctantly. As long as JP was here, I would be here too.

He arrived on the seventh day, and the first I knew of it was when JP reached out and grasped at my arm. I'd rather drifted off, I must admit, but as soon as JP grabbed, I was alert. There he was. He was walking past the pub, calmly; perhaps he imagined that no one would recognise him, just as they had failed to do when he was in hiding. JP got up from his chair straight away – a little awkwardly, I noticed, he was still not back to full strength – and headed for the door. I followed him. JP had made me promise not to, but as I went out into the street, I thought: I should have brought a weapon.

Gray had reached the door to his apartment building by the time we got out on the street, and, before I could think twice, I called out his name. He turned round. He did not appear shocked to see us. I'm trying to remember how long we stood there. You'd think, after everything JP has told me about memory, that I would be careful to remember the details and be precise. But I'm not sure.

Gray spoke first. 'You're not going to say anything, JP? Even now?' His lips curled. 'How arrogant. How typical.' His face was different. Harsher. The eyes. The mouth.

It was I who spoke next. 'The police have a record of everything that's happened,' I said. My voice sounded thin and weak.

Gray didn't even glance at me. He kept looking at his old friend. 'I can be silent too JP,' he said. 'I can use the same *tactic,* the same strategy to control and manipulate people. I can be silent about everything that's important. No confession, or admission, or explanation.' He tapped his lips with his forefinger. 'Silence,' he said, and his lips curled again. 'How do *you* like it?'

Gray must have made some kind of movement. I must have thought that he was going to turn and run. I ran forward and grabbed his arm. I don't remember what I said, or how he reacted, or what he said in return – *oh, the unreliability of memories* – but I know we began to struggle and he hit me in the face and I hit him back. It was over quickly though. Gray is much stronger than I am. In the brief struggle that followed, I fell against JP, who toppled over, his stick clattering on the paving stones, and in the moment that I turned towards JP, Gray wrestled free of my grip and ran down the street. I called after him. I called for the police. Faces began appearing at the windows of the buildings around us. But there was no hope of catching Gray. Our vigil had been a stupid idea from the start and it had ended with the prey escaping. I remember what I thought as I helped JP to his feet: *we have learned nothing.*

29

I have told you the story of what happened to Miss Sarah Brindle and now I must tell you how it ends. It ends with a funeral. JP and I took a long time to decide whether we should attend. To be frank, I think there was a part of me that suspected Gray wasn't really dead. Over the last few months, we had lived with several illusions about death. The illusion of Sarah Brindle being stabbed to death in front of JP and Gray. The illusion of Gray being killed by a tram, and being identified by his mother in the morgue, and being buried in the graveyard. Maybe this was an illusion too. So why go to a funeral if it could all turn out to be another lie?

But there could be no doubt this time. There were dozens of witnesses. After our confrontation with Gray in the street outside his apartment, he and Mrs R had finally tried to put their plan to flee abroad into action. We found out afterwards that they had sent their bags on ahead, under assumed names. The plan was then to take a train to Southampton and from there a ship to the United States. Their papers said they were Mrs Agatha Swale, widow, and her nephew, Mr William Frith.

But by now, the police – who for so long, it seemed to me, had never taken JP's theory very seriously – were finally closing in on Gray and Mrs R. They knew of their plans. They knew which train they intended to take, and they set a trap. There were officers placed at strategic points outside the railway station and within. The plan was to move in as soon as Gray and Mrs R arrived at the entrance to the station and arrest them. But it did not go according to plan. Gray and Mrs R arrived at the front of the station by cab. Three groups of police officers then stepped from the hiding places and began to move in. Mrs

R, as the cab drew away, saw the officers approaching and would have known at once what was happening.

The accounts of what happened next vary slightly, but the constables who were moving in agree on the important facts. Mrs R seemed to hesitate for a minute, before turning to her son. Gray was standing with his back to her, watching as more officers crossed the road towards them. He, too, would have known their time was up. The constables told us Mrs R took a step towards her son, and with a strength which it didn't look like she possessed, and before any of the constables could intervene, she put up her hands, her thin, pale hands, and pushed her son, quickly, firmly, into the road. It was over in a second, we were told, and the sound, apparently, was hellish. Mrs R had pushed Gray into the path of a tram. He died under the wheels. *Those who sleep in death will be raised.* Lies become truth.

The funeral was brief, and bleak. Gray was buried in a far corner of the graveyard and the gravediggers removed the stone that had been placed over the resting place of the stranger and placed it over the grave of JP's former friend. The words on the marble were not changed. *Though worms destroy this body yet in my flesh shall I see God.* I wondered how JP might be at the funeral, how upset he might be, but he appeared to be completely calm. He still had his walking stick. I wasn't sure whether he still needed it, but he lent on it slightly as he read the inscription. Then he turned away and started walking up the hill.

It was at the second funeral that I shed my first tear. JP paid for the stone to be carved and arranged for a priest to perform the service. This was the place where we thought Gray had been buried. It was the place where Mrs R had cried for the son that was not dead, and I was glad that we could, in a small way, correct the deception. I hoped as well that we could restore some of the dead man's dignity, although we still did not know his name. JP hadn't told me the words he'd chosen for the stone, and when I saw them, I realised that they were right. *A son, known to God.*

I did not know at that point that JP was planning another, final ceremony. In the days following the services at the graveyard, we learned that Mrs R would be charged with various offences of deception and perverting the course of justice as well as the murder of her son. Perhaps the trial would answer the questions that were still unanswered, although I doubted it. What had Mrs R known about Gray? She had perpetrated the deception of his death to protect him, but was she protecting a drug addict, or a drug addict *and* a murderer? Had she known from the beginning that Gray killed Sarah Brindle? In a way, it didn't seem to much matter now. She would have done whatever she thought was necessary to protect her son, including her last act of violence and love: sending him to meet his God.

The final act of remembrance happened about two weeks later. JP wrote to me and said he wanted to take me out, somewhere that might chase away the remnants of the tension and concern we'd been feeling for months. He suggested the theatre and told me in his letter that he had tickets arranged for the following Friday. It crossed my mind, of course, that the place where Sarah Brindle had died was perhaps an odd choice, but JP insisted.

When I arrived at the theatre, the first person I saw wasn't JP but Miss Elizabeth Mackie, the nurse. I was pleased to see her. For a while, we stood in the foyer and talked over recent events and it was only after quite a few minutes that we realised Miss Mackie had also been invited by JP. She showed me her ticket. We were seated in the same box. She then seemed to notice something over my shoulder and raised her hand in greeting.

It was the twins, Barbara and Rachel. They were coming through the doors into the foyer. Barbara noticed us first and came over and kissed Miss Mackie on the cheek and shook my hand; Rachel, as usual, was a little shyer but seemed pleased to see us. A couple of minutes later, Daniel arrived; he too had been invited by JP. I still remembered my first encounter with him, not far from here, when his face had been fired up with anger, but tonight he was smiling and friendly. 'We've all been invited by JP then?' he said.

We had been standing around in the foyer for some time, waiting I suppose for JP himself, when one of the ushers approached us. 'This way, ladies and gentlemen,' he said. He pointed to a corridor leading from the foyer and we followed him along until we reached the box. JP was already there, standing just inside. The walking stick was gone. I noticed that first, although I could still see a certain stiffness when he moved. He was almost completely recovered, I thought: *physically*. I was pleased to see him and he seemed pleased to see his friends. He came up to us one by one and shook our hands and kissed the ladies on the cheek. I had never quite seen him like this before. From the moment I'd met him at university all those months ago and tried to speak to him in the corridor, he had always seemed to have a melancholy, rather, haunted expression on his face. And the silence. It had always been a barrier, a kind of wall. But tonight, I thought that perhaps a small change had come over JP; I thought, perhaps, that some of his melancholia had lifted.

My thoughts were interrupted by Miss Mackie. She was speaking to JP. 'Was this you?' she said. 'Is this why you brought us here?' She put her hand up to her mouth and I could see that she'd started to weep. Barbara came forward and put her arm round Miss Mackie, which is when she noticed it too. It was a plaque on the wall. I moved forward so that I could read it and I realised what JP had done. This was the final ceremony. This, after those terrible, bleak services in the graveyard, was JP's most important act of remembrance. The plaque was brass, polished, the words picked out in black. It read: *THE SARAH BRINDLE ROOM. In memory of Miss Sarah Brindle, actress, with the gratitude of all her friends.*

I turned to JP. He was standing observing his friends, his back to the audience. The theatre was filling with people. In the orchestra pit, the musicians were warming up. The atmosphere was warm and exciting; suddenly there seemed to be so much *noise*. I was about to say something about his wonderful, unexpected tribute, JP's act of remembrance to Sarah, when he put his hand out and grasped my arm. I looked into his face and could see that my first impression had been wrong – the melancholia wasn't gone; how could it be? I suddenly couldn't think of anything to say. But it didn't matter. Silence was our language now and always had been. I put my hand on top of his, and a striking thought occurred to me. There was some other quality in JP's face that made me think it. I suddenly believed, I knew, there and then, standing in the box of the theatre, with all the noise around me, that my friend, my eccentric, frustrating, wonderful, silent friend, the man who would come to be known to so many as the silent detective, was about to say his very first words to me.

AUTHOR'S NOTE

If you would like to read more about the First World War, and some of the issues covered in What He Never Said, you might like the following books.

We Will Not Fight: The Untold Story of World War One's Conscientious Objectors by Will Ellsworth-Jones

Six Weeks: The Short and Gallant Life of the British Officer in the First World War by John Lewis-Stempel

Mud, Blood and Poppycock: Britain and the Great War by Gordon Corrigan

Out in the Army by James Wharton

Mark Findlay Smith is a writer, journalist, and columnist for The Herald. His short story Perce was a winner of the SFX Pulp Fiction award and The Man on the Phone is published by Big Finish in Short Trips. You can email him at markfindlaysmith@gmail.com

Printed in Great Britain
by Amazon